Trail of Gold

Fascinating Stories of Adventure in Early California Based on Historical Truth

by ELISE FRASER

Published by

These stories with the exception of "The Chinese Jinx" were published first in "Youth's Story Paper." "The Chinese Jinx" was published in "Young People's Paper."

Printed in the U. S. A.

To the members and friends of The Torch Club, young adult group, of St. Paul's United Presbyterian Church, Berkeley, California, who first suggested that these stories be collected and put into a book.

CONTENTS

Mystery of Moaning Cave 7
San Diego during the period of the Mexican War 1846-1848

The Green Treasure Box 27
The story of Wells Fargo "money box" in the days of stage coach robberies, etc. 1853

The Chinese Jinx 63
The story of "Parrott's Castle" and the jinx put on it by the Chinese. (Parrott's Castle was the home of Wells Fargo for 70 years) 1854

Christmas at Lone Pine Inn 83
The Sierras—1850

Mystery of Moaning Cave

1 UNDER THE scorching heat of mid-afternoon, in July of the year 1846, the tricolored flag of old Mexico hung limp above the plaza of the village of San Diego. The deep, blue waters of San Diego Bay were calm and unruffled. No wind was stirring.

On a hillside, covered with scrub oaks and manzanita, two boys stood looking out over the crescent-shaped bay. One was fair skinned with light brown hair and blue eyes, the other was dark skinned, with black hair and brown eyes. The blonde lad was named Daniel Bennett and his companion was Miguel, an Indian.

The two boys were having an argument, for Miguel wanted to crawl under a scrub oak, pull his wide-brimmed sombrero over his face and go to sleep. But Dan wanted to explore. So far Dan had managed to keep Miguel awake by reminding him that the caverns of Moaning Cave were cool and dark. Indeed, in some places the walls of the cave were damp and covered with a slimy green that might be moss. And besides, wasn't there a chance that there was treasure in the cave? Buried treasure?

"How many years ago was it that the great ship sailed into the waters of this bay?" Dan asked.

"How many, I do not know," Miguel responded. "But my grandfather said that the ship was like a huge bird with great white wings."

"And your grandfather saw the captain and his men carry a chest to Moaning Cave?" Dan questioned.

Miguel nodded. "He saw them go to the cave with the chest and come away with nothing. It was by moonlight and my grandfather and his people watched from behind the shrubs."

"And you're sure your grandfather never found the chest?"

"Yes, I'm sure. He looked for it but he never found it. And the men in the boat that was like a huge bird with great white wings never came again."

"It was a Spanish ship," Dan said knowingly, "trading with the Islands in the Pacific. Maybe the chest was filled with gold or maybe pearls. We must find it, Miguel!"

"The men were kind," Miguel said. "My grandfather liked them. At first my people were afraid and hid themselves. But the men made signs that they would be friends and my grandfather went to them. They made known to him that they wanted fresh water and food and my grandfather and his people gave them what they needed. The men built a fire on the shore and roasted meat and ate it. They went away and although my grandfather watched for the ship like a great white bird, it never came again."

"Maybe pirates took the ship," Dan said, "or maybe the men died of fever."

"Who knows?" Miguel said. "My grandfather saw the white man no more in his generation. But when my father had grown to manhood there were many white people. The missionaries came and my people became Christians. My father liked it better when the Spanish flag was over Alta California. My father does not like the Mexican governor, Pio Pica."

"Many do not," Dan agreed. Dan turned his face away

from the blue waters of the bay to the crest of the hill. "A short cut to the cave is over the cliff. Shall we try it?"

"It is nothing," Miguel answered. "I have gone up and down the cliff many times."

"You are brave, Miguel," Dan said. "But if you can do it, I can do it."

Clinging to rocks and shrubs, the boys cautiously lowered themselves down the steep cliff. Below them were great boulders, the sands of the shoreline and the mighty stretches of the Pacific. Concealed behind the rocks was the entrance to Moaning Cave. The cave had been given its name because of the strange moaning sounds which could be heard inside the narrow caverns.

"It is strange that your father has never searched for the treasure of Moaning Cave, Miguel."

"Maybe he did when he was a lad. But he says now that the only treasure he seeks is the treasure in the Holy Bible. He constantly thanks the Lord Jesus that the missionaries taught him to read and also that your father gave him a copy of the Book. He reads it night and morning. For 'What greater treasure,' says he, 'can a man find than the gift of eternal life!' "

"We, too, have family worship in the morning and evening," Dan said. "Father says that when we live among so many people who do not remember the Lord's Day to keep it holy, we must fortify ourselves with Scripture reading and daily prayer."

When they stepped into the cave, Miguel gave a sigh of relief. "Ah, it is cool here."

The floor of the cave was covered with wet sand. When the tide was in the waves of the ocean swept up as far as the opening.

"Father said there is another entrance to this cave." Miguel spoke thoughtfully as he and Dan walked cautiously forward.

"Let's try to find it," Dan suggested.

Miguel shook his head. "It's not safe to go too far into the cave. There are dangers there," Father said.

For some distance the cave seemed to cut straight ahead into the rock. In the dim light from the entrance, the boys looked at the walls carefully, hoping to find some niche in which the treasure chest might repose. But the walls, though rough, held no hiding places. After a stretch of about fifty feet, the cave narrowed and Dan and Miguel had to stoop and finally to crawl on their hands and knees. After a time they came to a place where the narrow tunnel divided into two passages. "Let's keep to the right," Miguel said.

They soon found themselves in total darkness. Dan turned but could not see so much as a speck of light in any direction.

"Miguel," Dan whispered, "maybe we'd better go back!"

"Better go back!" sounded the hollow echo of Dan's voice.

"Yes," Miguel agreed. "Let's go back."

It seemed to Dan that he had crawled on his hands and knees for more than an hour but they did not come to the wider cave, or see the light of the entrance.

"Listen!" Dan cried, fear gripping his heart.

The cave was filled with a mighty roaring.

"The tide's in," Miguel whispered. "That's the ocean beating against the rocks. Now we'll have to stay in here or find the other entrance."

"Let's pray that the Lord Jesus will lead us to the entrance. Do you believe He will, Miguel?"

"He will do what is best for us, whatever that is," Miguel answered.

After he and Miguel had prayed, Dan felt better. "We'll wait till the tide rolls back, Miguel. Let's talk. Did you know that there is a war being fought?"

"No. What war is that?"

"The United States is at war with Mexico. My father told me. There are great battles going on across the mountains in Texas and in Mexico. If the United States wins against Mexico they will take Alta (Upper) California."

"Will you like that?" Miguel asked.

"Oh, yes. My family would like it. Juan Bandini would like it, too, even though he is a subject of Mexico. He favors it strongly, in secret, of course. His daughters, Josefa, Ysabel and Arcadia Bandini made an American flag. I saw it myself, Miguel, and it is beautiful! It is made of red and blue flannel and white muslin sheets. My father says that the day the American flag flies over the village of San Diego, he will give me the beautiful white pony, Stardust . . ."

Dan stopped short, for to his astonishment he heard what sounded like a muffled sneeze. His thin fingers clenched Miguel's arm. "Did you sneeze, Miguel?"

"No," whispered Miguel. "It is someone in the cave. There is someone right here! Sh!"

"Hello! Who's there?" Dan called.

"Hello! Who's there?" his voice echoed back.

And then came silence. All Dan heard was the roar of the waves against the cave. He wished he had not spoken so freely about Juan Bandini and the American flag his daughters were making. But who would have supposed that anyone else would be in the cave?

Suddenly there was a dim light in the cave and then darkness.

"What was that?" Dan asked.

"I feel better," Miguel replied. "Know what that was? Somebody opened and shut a door right ahead of us. It must be the other entrance Father told me about."

Cautiously, Dan crawled forward. Miguel was close behind. The cave began to widen. Dan found that he could now stand on his feet. He raised his hands but could not touch the ceiling. "This must be like a room, Miguel, even bigger than the other end of the cave."

"Yes, we must find the door."

It was Dan who first touched the wood and then pushed on the door. It swung open, creaking on its rusty hinges. Dan exclaimed with surprise as he recognized the rancho on which the door opened. It belonged to the Machados, a family loyal to Mexico and who disliked the "Gringos," as the Americans were called. An Indian servant, probably the one who had been in the cave, was walking swiftly toward the house.

2

IT WAS late that night when Dan reached Casa de Bennett, as his home was called. He was eager to tell Father of his adventures in Moaning Cave. But as soon as Dan entered the house, he saw that there was a guest. The whole household seemed very much excited. Judging from Mother's smile and shining eyes, Dan thought the guest must have brought good news.

Dan was introduced to the man whose name was Jeremiah Cartwright. Senor Cartwright had bushy red hair and a long red beard. His cheeks were red, too, and his eyes were very blue. He was a traveler on the King's Highway. Ten days ago he had left Monterey.

"Senor Cartwright brings good news from Monterey, Son!" Father said.

Jeremiah Cartwright beamed at Dan. "Great news, my boy! The American flag was raised on California soil on July 7, in this year of our Lord, 1846. In a great speech Commandant Sloat proclaimed California a part of the United States and the Star and Stripes were hoisted over the custom house at Monterey. Not an opposing voice was raised. The people cheered wildly. Ah! It was a great sight. 'Tis said that the American vessel *Cyane* is now on the way to San Diego."

"Let's hope all goes equally well in San Diego," was all Mother said.

Father nodded in approval. "The majority will rejoice to see the American flag in the old plaza. But some may cause trouble. The Machados, I fear, will not stand by and see their beloved flag lowered."

Father and Senor Cartwright discussed the reasons why Californians wanted American rule. They needed the protection of the United States for one thing, for they were not strong enough to be an independent nation. And they preferred American rule as this would mean that public schools would be opened, there would be better government, business would flourish, the country would develop. Dan grew more and more sleepy and finally said he would go to bed. So Father said they would have Scripture reading and prayers.

With the Scripture in his mind, "I will both lay me down in peace, and sleep: for thou, Lord, only makest me dwell in safety," Dan felt happy and comfortable in his bed and was soon sound asleep.

He was awakened by his Mother's voice singing. "The Lord's my Shepherd, I'll not want," she sang and Dan knew a new day had begun, for that was Mother's favorite hymn.

It was a beautiful day. The sky was blue. The red roses climbing up the adobe walls of the house sent their sweet fragrance through the open casement windows. The pepper tree in the patio was motionless in the calm morning air. Dan heard the cheerful notes of the meadow larks, chickadees and robins. He heard the blue jays scolding. From the kitchen came the cheerful voices of the Indian women as they worked, preparing the tortillas for the day.

Dan knew that Father had come to California before Dan was born. He had taken a sea voyage for his health, sailing on a trading vessel from Boston. The vessel made the adventurous trip around the Horn to the coast of California. Arriving in the harbor of San Diego Bay, Senor

Bennett saw that a lively business was being done by the Californians in the sale of hides to the trading vessels. And hides were easy to procure for oxen and cattle were thick on the hills. There were wild horses, too, in abundance. The hides sold for two dollars each and in exchange the trading vessels brought household items, cloth for garments, silks and cottons, and handy tools.

Senor Bennett liked the sunny climate of San Diego, the beautiful bay and the hills. He saw that it was a land of great richness. There was fruit of every variety, vegetables and grain in abundance. Turkeys, chickens, geese and quail were plentiful. The waters teemed with fish of many kinds. There was wool from sheep.

And California was not entirely cut off from the world, for supplies for the settlers came from Mazatlan on the Mexican coast and then, even more important, were the Yankee ships from Boston.

And so Senor Bennett had decided to become a settler in California and to engage in the trading of hides. His happiness was complete when a missionary family arrived in San Diego. The missionary traveled the King's Highway, preaching the gospel of the Lord Jesus Christ. Senor Bennett soon fell in love with the missionary's oldest daughter whom he married. So Dan was born into a fine Christian home. Dan was happy, too, in having a sister. Matilda was three years older than Dan, who was twelve. Matilda no longer played like a child. She was a young lady.

Dan stretched, yawned, and then got dressed. He was excited as he looked forward to this day, for had not his father promised him the beautiful white pony, Stardust, when the American flag was raised over San Diego? And had not Senor Cartwright said that the American vessel, *Cyane,* was bound for San Diego for the express purpose of raising the Stars and Stripes over the old plaza?

Dan had hardly finished his breakfast before a rider came to Casa de Bennett bringing the news that an American sloop-of-war was sailing into the waters of San Diego Bay. Such excitement as there was in the household! Senor Jeremiah Cartwright who had planned to leave that day decided to stay to see the great happenings in San Diego. Matilda hurried over to the home of her friends, Josefa, Ysabel and Arcadia Bandini that they might go together to the plaza.

Dan went to find Miguel. He looked for him in the kitchen and he wasn't there. He looked for him in the courtyard and in the stable. And then he looked for him in his bed and there he was, fast asleep.

"Wake up, wake up, lazy bones!" Dan cried as he shook Miguel.

Miguel leaped up. "What is it?" he asked. "Have you found the treasure of Moaning Cave?"

"No, not yet," Dan answered. He had forgotten the treasure in the present excitement. "The *Cyane* has sailed into San Diego Bay and everyone goes to the plaza to see the American flag raised over the plaza."

Miguel did not seem to think the event half so important as the treasure of Moaning Cave, but he obediently dressed. On the way out he passed through the kitchen that he might grab a tortilla to eat on the way.

A great crowd of people had already gathered on Presidio Hill and Dan and Miguel wove in and out through the crowd until they had a good view of the bay. They saw the American vessel, *Cyane,* anchored near Ballast Point. A number of small boats filled with marines had been lowered and were now approaching the shore. There was an officer in one of the boats, too. From the whisperings among the people, Dan learned that the officer was Lieutenant Rowan.

When the marines came ashore carrying a large American flag, a great shout went up from the people, "Vivan los Americanos!" (Long live the Americans.) Dan and Miguel shouted with all the rest.

The marines marched to the plaza and everyone hurried to join them. Lieutenant Rowan read the proclamation which said that California was now a part of the United States. The people must be loyal to their new government. Then he gave an order that the Mexican flag be lowered and the American flag raised over the old plaza. Again the people cheered, "Vivan los Americanos!" Dan's heart beat wildly as Old Glory floated for the first time above the village of San Diego. Dan was glad that all went well and that no one seemed to object to the new flag and the new government.

But as the crowd broke up, Dan saw dark looks on the faces of some. He heard an undercurrent of murmurings. He saw the Machados with sullen faces. All this worried Dan. But he soon forgot his worry when he remembered Father's promise that he was to have the pony, Stardust, when the American flag was raised over San Diego. Dan hurried home to claim his prize, Miguel following close beside him.

Not only did Father make good his promise to give Dan the pony but he also gave him a beautiful silver-studded saddle! And Father did even more. He gave Miguel a lively little black pony, Kino, so that the boys might ride together. Dan liked that, for he was very, very fond of Miguel.

The summer days were long and pleasant. Dan and Miguel spent hours riding Stardust and Kino over the trails. The treasure of Moaning Cave was forgotten—almost.

Everything was quiet in San Diego. The *Cyane* had sailed away. Then there came a rumor to trouble the people. It was said that Andres Pica, brother of Pio Pica, the former governor, who had fled Monterey when the American flag was raised there, had gathered a great company of men and were marching toward Los Angeles to capture the city. They would come to San Diego, too, and there were but six American soldiers in the village left to guard the flag.

Don Machado, too, they said, was plotting trouble. But what trouble, no one knew.

Early one morning Dan awoke to hear a great commotion in the house. He thought surely that the Mexicans had come. Then he heard the Indian servants wailing. Someone was shouting and Dan ran out to the courtyard to see what it was all about.

"The horses! The horses! They've been stolen! All the horses are gone!" The servants ran here and there looking for the missing animals.

Dan ran quickly to the stables for he could not believe that all the horses were gone. But the stables were empty! Stardust was gone and Miguel's pony, Kino, was gone, too.

3

DAN AND Miguel were heart-broken when they discovered that Stardust and Kino were gone. The Indian servants, gathered in little groups in the courtyard, were saying that the Mexicans had stolen all the horses so that the people of San Diego would not be able to escape. From the north and the south and the east, the Mexicans were marching toward the village and the Americans had but six soldiers to defend the town.

Dan and Miguel ran off to see if other stables, too, were empty. Sure enough, all the horses in the village had been stolen. As the boys passed the Casa de Bandini, they saw Josefa, Ysabel and Arcadia placing the American flag they had made in the window. The crowd in the street cheered when they saw the flag, saying, "Vivan los Americanos!"

Dan noticed a group of men talking earnestly about the stolen horses. They were saying, "There's no doubt that the Machados are the leaders in this."

Dan nudged Miguel. "Moaning Cave," he whispered. "We'll find those horses. We'll take candles with us and matches for striking fire. We will take a little food also in case we should get lost and be hungry."

Dan and Miguel hurried to Casa de Bennett. No one noticed Dan as he gathered up what he needed from the kitchen. The boys filled their pockets and set out for the cliff which was a short-cut to the cave. Cautiously, they climbed down the steep precipice, clinging to the shrubs which grew in the crevices of the rock. Soon they were inside Moaning Cave.

Dan lighted two candles, one for himself and one for Miguel, and walked slowly through the cave. Before long they reached the place where the cave narrowed and the ceiling was low so that they had to crawl on hands and knees. It was hard to crawl along the floor and to hold the candle, too, but the boys were managing very well until suddenly a strong gust of wind rushed through the rocky cavern, snuffed out the candles, and left the boys in sudden darkness.

"Someone must have opened that door," whispered Miguel, "and that sent the wind through the cave."

"That is strange," Dan said. "How quickly we have come. We were longer on the way before. Did we take a different turn? Let's light our candles again so that we can see where we are."

Shielding their candles, Dan lighted them again. The candles sputtered and gave a feeble light in the blackness of the cave. Then Miguel gave a cry of terror. "Look!" he cried. Miguel's finger pointed downward and Dan looked to see that the floor of the cave ended abruptly only two feet away. At the edge of the floor was a deep pit. Now and then the wind, with a sighing sound like a low moan, swept through the narrow passage. "It was this wind that put out our candles," Dan said, "not the open door to the Machados!"

Holding their candles over the edge of the pit, Dan and Miguel looked into it. There was a stream at the bottom which made a gurgling sound as it rippled over and around the rocks.

Dan whistled softly. "Another step and we might have fallen into the pit. Let's thank our Heavenly Father for keeping us safe, Miguel."

"Yes," Miguel replied, "and let's keep our candles burning."

Dan was staring with fascination into the deep pit. There were rocks and boulders, around and between which a man might descend in a circular course to the bottom.

"Let's see what this pit is like," Dan said.

The boys began cautiously to climb around the rocks. To their surprise, at the bottom they saw that there was another tunnel through the cave below the level of the one they had left. A small stream flowed through this chasm. On either side there were dry rocks where they might walk.

The walls of the cavern were wet and clammy, coated in some places with a dark green fungus. After walking about a hundred feet through the tunnel, the boys found a large break in the wall about three feet above the floor. Curious, Dan and Miguel held up their candles to peer deep into the gloomy recess of the wall. With a startled exclamation, Dan drew back. For the opening revealed a small room, the floor of which was littered with dry, white bones!

Miguel continued to stare into the recess. "This must have been a burying place for my people," Miguel said. "Or maybe they sacrificed to their gods before the light of the gospel came to them."

Dan shivered. "I'm glad I'm a Christian, aren't you, Miguel?"

"Oh, yes," Miguel replied, "for now we do not walk in darkness." He seemed to be lost in thought. Suddenly he said slowly, "Maybe the men in the ship like a great white bird put their treasure in this room. My people would never come here to disturb the bones of the dead."

Miguel gave his candle to Dan. "Hold the candle so I can see, Dan. I'm going to climb into the room."

"When you're in, take the candles," Dan said. "I can be as brave as you are."

Inside the opening, Miguel pointed to a pile of stones in the corner of the room. "Maybe under these stones, the men in the ship like a great white bird buried their treasure!"

Dan and Miguel began to move the pile of rocks one by one. "Look, Miguel, look!" Dan exclaimed. "It is the Spanish treasure chest!"

Sure enough, under the rocks was a battered, iron-bound chest, securely padlocked. Dan and Miguel tried to move it but it would not budge.

"It must weigh a ton," Dan said.

Miguel stared at the chest. But the boys could neither move it nor open it.

"We must leave it here," Dan said at last. "We must wait until someone can come to help us open it."

"Let us cover it up again then," Miguel said.

The boys replaced the rocks, and climbed to the upper passage. But they could not remember the way they had come! Now what could they do? Praying that the Lord Jesus would lead them, they stumbled along the passage. Again they were in darkness. A gust of wind had blown out their candles and Dan had no more matches.

Realizing that they were lost, the boys clung together, not knowing which way to go. Then they heard the sound of shuffling feet and a whispered conversation of men. There was a heavy bang as of a door shutting and a grinding sound as if a heavy bolt had been slipped in place. The sound seemed to be only a few feet away.

"The wooden door," Dan whispered.

When they heard no further sound of voices and were convinced the men had left the cave, they crawled in the direction of the banging door. They found themselves in the larger cave from which the door opened. They knew their way now! After feeling around in the darkness, they found the door. But it would not open. It was heavily bolted from the outside.

"I'm hungry," Miguel said.

"So'm I," Dan admitted.

The boys reached in their pockets and pulled out the tortillas they had stuffed there. They were munching contentedly when they heard the neigh of a horse.

"Stardust!" Dan cried. "That's Stardust!" He ran to the door and tried with all his might to open it. But it would not give way. Miguel, too, pushed against it. But it was secure.

"Let's go and tell Father that we've found Stardust," Dan said.

"And the Spanish treasure chest," Miguel added.

"Remember to keep to the right," Dan cautioned as they started back to the ocean entrance of the cave. It was dusk when the boys climbed the cliff.

They were hurrying toward the plaza when Dan, who was in the lead, stopped abruptly. He jumped behind the bushes, pulling Miguel with him. The plaza was filled with Mexican soldiers. Not an American was in sight! And over the village of San Diego flew, not the Stars and Stripes, but the tricolored flag of Mexico.

Dan and Miguel looked at each other in astonishment. How could all this have been accomplished so suddenly? They had heard no sound of battle, no report of gun fire. But was this because they were deep in the cave?

Where were the American soldiers? Where was his father and mother and Matilda?

"Oh, Miguel" Dan sobbed, "let's pray that the Americans are safe. Let's pray hard."

4 DARKNESS CAME quickly. Dan and Miguel were still hiding in the brush. They could hear the shouts and laughter of Mexican soldiers, the rattle of cups as they drank wine, no doubt in celebration of their easy victory.

Dan could wait no longer to go home to see if his family were safe. Miguel said it was not wise to go through the camp of the Mexicans until they slept, and that might be for some hours yet. So Dan agreed with Miguel — they decided to descend the cliff again and to take the long way around.

When they reached the shore, Miguel said, "Hark! Listen!"

Through the still night came the faint sound of muffled oars. The boys pressed close to the cliff, waiting. They heard the scraping sound of a boat being pulled up on the sands. And then in the starlight they saw the figure of a man move cautiously toward the cliff. As he drew nearer, Dan recognized the man as Albert Smith, an American, who like Dan's father worked with the hides.

"Senor Smith," Dan called softly.

With an exclamation of surprise, Albert Smith hurried toward the boys. "What are you doing here?" he demanded.

"Where are the Americans?" Dan asked. "Where are my parents and my sister?"

"They are safe." Albert Smith pointed out to the bay. "Safe on that whaling vessel anchored yonder."

When Albert Smith heard that the boys were ignorant of the happenings of the day, he told them what had taken place. Captain Merritt of the United States Army had come from San Luis Rey to defend the village of San Diego. But he had only sixteen men.

Captain Merritt was sure that the other Americans would send them help. But until help came they were too few in number to defend the city. He suggested that they take refuge on the whaling vessel until help would come.

But when they were all safe on the whaling boat, they

realized that they had forgotten to spike the guns in the fort. If the Mexicans thought of it, they could turn the guns on the ship and blow it to bits. So Albert Smith had come ashore to spike the guns. He showed the boys the hammer and spikes.

"Wait a little," Miguel advised. "When the Mexicans sleep, you may safely spike the guns." The boys told how the Mexicans were drinking to celebrate their victory. "Soon they will sleep soundly," Miguel added.

At the foot of the cliff, the three waited. When they could no longer hear the laughter and the singing of the Mexicans, they began to climb. Dan and Miguel went ahead, showing Albert Smith the safest way.

When they reached the camp of the sleeping Mexicans, Albert Smith quickly spiked the guns in the fort.

The three then returned to the whaling vessel. Mother embraced and kissed Dan, saying she had been told he was safe with the women and children at Casa de Estudillo.

"Children!" Dan scoffed. "I'm a man now. Am I not twelve years old?"

When Captain Merritt heard how the Mexicans were drinking, he suggested, "Now is the time for us to attack. Even if our men are only a handful, they are stronger than a great army that drinks wine."

At dawn, the boats were lowered. Captain Merritt with his soldiers and all the valiant Americans and Spanish Americans rowed ashore. Dan and Miguel went, too.

When the Mexicans saw the American soldiers lining up against them, they lined up, too. Dan thought they looked very fierce. Dan and Miguel were both praying that the battle would be soon over and that the Americans would be victorious.

To Dan's surprise, when the first shot was fired, the Mexican line broke up and the men scattered to the hills like a lot of frightened rabbits. The Americans shouted joyously, for they had won without a battle.

Crowds began to assemble in the plaza. Women and children from Casa de Estudillo ran to the plaza, too, where they all watched the Mexican flag being lowered. When it was nearly to the ground, Maria Machado ran out and gathered her beloved flag to her heart. No one stopped her for they all admired the brave spirit of the girl.

Then Captain Merritt said, "Who will climb the pole and secure the American flag?"

"Albert Smith!" the crowd shouted.

"No one better deserves the privilege," Captain Merritt answered.

With a big grin, Albert Smith put the flag over his shoulder and climbed the pole. A shot rang out as a sniper tried to hit him. But Albert Smith waved his hat and the crowd cheered. When the flag was safely secured, Senor Smith slid down the pole.

Again the Stars and Stripes floated over the village of San Diego. Again the people shouted, "Vivan los Americanos!" This time the flag was there to stay.

Next day Dan and Miguel watched a splendid American vessel sail into San Diego Bay. It was the United States frigate, *Congress* bringing Commodore Robert F. Stockton, commander-in-chief and governor of the Territory of California. He was welcomed joyfully.

But even in all the excitement, Dan did not forget his beloved horse, Stardust, or the treasure of Moaning Cave. He tried to tell Father about them but Senor Bennett was helping Don Bandini entertain the governor. He said that the horses and the treasure would have to wait.

But Dan wanted Stardust and Miguel wanted Kino. So early one morning the boys started out over the hills to Rancho de Machado. From the top of the hill they looked down on a long building which was used as a shed. It had a deserted look.

The boys slid down the hill. At the base they waited, listening intently for any sound, but everything was still.

They looked through the windows of the long shed which were only openings in the wall, without glass. The building was empty.

Then Dan heard a sound which made his heart beat faster. It was the sound of a neigh and it was very familiar. "Stardust!" Dan cried. "Miguel, it's Stardust!"

Dan ran around the shed with Miguel close at his heels.

"Stardust! Stardust!" Dan cried.

"Kino! Kino!" Miguel shouted.

Again they heard the neigh, nearer this time.

Stumbling over the rough ground, they came to a thick patch of tangled brambles, higher than their heads. Not minding the scratches, they pushed their way through. There they found the horses, hidden in a little valley surrounded on three sides by sheer, rocky cliffs.

Dan threw his arms around Stardust's neck and Miguel embraced Kino. "Stardust!" "Kino!" How glad they were to find their beloved horses.

"But how can we get them out?" Miguel asked. "We can't go up that rocky cliff. To go out we must pass Casa de Machado."

"Then we must go by the house," Dan said bravely.

"But suppose they stop us?" Miguel said.

"Let's draw near the house to see what we find," Dan said.

So the boys went to investigate. But the house, too, looked deserted. Only an old Indian dozed in a chair in the courtyard. So the boys returned to the little valley, mounted Stardust and Kino and rode swiftly past Casa de Machado. The old Indian stirred but he did not wake up.

Dan's father praised the boys for bravery in recovering their horses. Indian servants were sent to bring the other horses back to their owners.

But the Mexican war was not ended yet. Now and then there came news of fighting in the valley, and in Los Angeles. But after a while the message came that the war was ended and California was at peace. The Stars and Stripes flew over the territory from Sonoma to San Diego. And to settle it, the United States government paid Mexico fifteen million dollars for the country north of the Rio Grande.

Every day Dan and Miguel rode over the hills with Stardust and Kino. But they did not forget the treasure of Moaning Cave. Sometimes they went to the cave to make sure the treasure was still safe. Some day they would open the chest and find it full of Spanish gold.

Finally the day came when Father listened and went with Dan and Miguel to see the treasure chest left by the men in the boat that was like a big white bird. He opened the chest. And it was just as Dan thought. The chest was filled with Spanish gold.

Mother smiled when Dan told her of the treasure. "Don't forget," she said, "that the greatest treasure is eternal life. To belong to the Lord Jesus is worth more than all the gold in all the wide world."

The Green Treasure Box

1 CAPTAIN JOSIAH Bartholomew put his arm over the shoulders of his cabin boy, Danny Winslow. He spoke very kindly. "I don't like to see you set out by yourself, Danny. A twelve-year-old boy might easily get into trouble in this gold-mad country of California."

Danny's clear blue eyes looked into the troubled brown eyes of the Captain. He had great respect for this tall, broad-shouldered man with bushy black hair. He did not like to do anything the Captain might object to. Still, he had his father's letter in his pocket.

Danny looked out over the blue waters of San Francisco Bay, sparkling in the sun. Deserted boats, small and large, were anchored there, all their crews gone off to the "diggings," as the gold mines were called.

"I'll be all right, Captain Barth!" Danny said eagerly. "Father said he would meet me in San Francisco unless something happened to prevent. If he didn't come, I was to take this letter to the Wells Fargo and Company express office in Columbia. They will tell me where to find him."

The Captain continued to look down at Danny. The troubled look in his eyes did not clear. "See these hundreds of boats, Danny? The sea is only one way the gold hunters come. They stream over the mountains, they come up from Mexico. They come from the north. Thousands of them. How can you hope to find your father in such mad confusion?"

For a moment Danny felt his confidence fail, then he said with assurance, "Father says that Wells Fargo and Company is the miner's best friend. You can depend on Wells Fargo, Father says."

"I've heard, too, the uncanny way in which they find the miners and deliver mail, and that gold is safe with them. So I hope your father is right and they can tell you where he is. Still, I'm troubled that he has not come to San Francisco for you. I don't like to say this, Danny, but something may have happened to him . . ."

"Oh, no!" Danny cried, frightened at this possibility.

"I don't say it *has,*" the Captain answered quickly. "But you are old enough now to look on the world with the eyes of a man."

"Mother and I have prayed every day that the Lord Jesus would keep Father safe," Danny said stoutly. "And Father prayed every day for us. He said so in his letter."

The Captain nodded. "Yes, Danny," he said gently, "when we belong to the Lord Jesus we are safe, whether rich or poor, well or sick, in this life or the next. I'm sure of that all right."

Danny wet his dry lips. "So I'm sure Father is well and safe," he said. But he faltered a bit as he spoke.

"Yes, Danny. No doubt he is. But still it is strange that he has not come to meet you. Wouldn't it be better for you to wait here on the boat for a few days? Your father might come then. Perhaps he has only been delayed. Or better, wait until some of our crew return from the diggings. They might have word of your father."

"No," Danny replied, "I cannot wait here. I must go to find my father."

"You have money, Danny? "

Danny patted his pocket. "Yes, here — in my wallet."

"Hang on to it, Danny. Honest men have come to search for gold but thieves and robbers have come to plunder. So watch out!"

"I'll be careful," Danny promised.

"I wish I could go with you," the Captain added. "But I must see if I can't get a crew together to take this boat back to Boston."

"Ha! Ha! Ha!" a hoarse laugh sounded near them.

Startled, Danny turned to see the ship's cook sitting on a coil of rope near them, laughing until his side shook.

The cook was called "Red" because of the color of his hair. It was thick and bushy and stood straight up in the air. Red Mitchell was only seventeen but in Danny's eyes he was a full-grown man.

"What's so funny?" the Captain demanded.

The cook pointed to all the abandoned ships and then to the flimsy structures along the waterfront, the San Francisco of the year 1853. "Who will go to sea when he can get rich overnight in the gold mines?"

"Money that comes easy, goes easy," said the Captain. "There may come a day, Red, when you'll be glad enough to work your passage home."

"Not me!" Red boasted. "I'll get rich in the mines, not cooking at sea."

The Captain looked at the cook with a strange, sharp look in his eyes. "You want to go to the diggings, Red? Why don't you go along with Danny? He'll take you to the heart of the gold country. That's where his father is."

"Not a bad idea!" Red said, jumping to his feet.

Danny was pleased. It would be good to have someone he knew along with him. So the two said good-by to Captain Bartholomew and prepared to leave the ship.

"Take care of Danny, Red," the Captain said. "And Danny you watch out for Red, too." Both promised as they started across the gangplank, waving farewell to the Captain.

The bowsprit of the ship hung over the narrow street. There were people everywhere, people of many races and of different nationalities. There were Chinese with long pigtails, carrying baskets on poles swung over their shoulders. There were swarthy Mexicans and Spaniards, dark-skinned Italians; there were Russians, Australians and Englishmen. And there were Yankees and men from the South. And interspersed with English talk were chats and talk in many foreign tongues.

"The first thing I have to do, Red, is to go to the post office. Maybe there's a letter from Father."

"You'll have to wait in line for weeks," Red said gloomily.

"Not weeks, maybe hours," Danny responded.

He felt new hope. Maybe there was some word for him from Father! As they walked along Montgomery Street, Danny's eyes were everywhere. The narrow street was lined with hotels, banks, stores, and saloons. At the end of the street was a steep hill. On the top of the hill was a semaphore which signaled the arrival of ships to the people of San Francisco. This hill was called Telegraph Hill.

It seemed to Danny that there were hundreds of people in front of the post office. There were men on horseback. There were miners wearing rough clothes and broad-brimmed hats. There were many merchants, women, and children. After a wait of several hours, it was Danny's turn to ask for mail. But there was no letter for him.

Danny's disappointment was so great that the tears came into his eyes. But he blinked them back bravely.

As he waited for Red to ask for his mail, Danny noticed a girl about his own age standing near. She had a basket over her arm. She lifted the lid and Danny saw a soft black kitten in the basket. "Don't be afraid, Tar Baby," the girl whispered.

The girl looked up, then smiled at Danny in a friendly way.

"That's a pretty little kitten," Danny said.

"Yes, isn't he? We brought his mother all the way from Boston."

"I'm from Boston, too!" Danny said cheerfully. But there was a tiny lump in his throat as he thought of home.

Just then there was a noise of thundering horses and a clanging of bells.

"Fire! Fire!"

The fire engine drawn by two horses raced by. The crowd broke and people began to run after the fire engine. But Danny heard a cry of distress right beside him.

"Oh, Tar Baby! They've frightened Tar Baby!"

Danny saw a black streak dart across the road. The fair-haired girl with the basket on her arm ran after it.

"I'll get him for you!" Danny shouted.

The kitten scurried away across the open road and Danny flew after him. Scrambling through yards and alleys, Danny managed to keep his eye on the little black kitten. But Danny's clothes were muddy and torn before he finally captured Tar Baby who had scrambled on top of a low roof for safety.

"Shame on you, Tar Baby," Danny said, "running away like that!"

He carried the squirming kitten back to his mistress.

"How can I thank you!" the girl cried. "I'll lock the lid securely this time so Tar Baby won't get away again." She smiled at Danny. "My name is Susanne Edwards."

"I'm Danny Winslow."

The girl smiled. "I hope I'll see you again some time, Danny. But maybe not. We are leaving today by steamboat for Sacramento. Thank you again for saving Tar Baby. Good-by and God bless you."

Danny stared after Susanne. How gentle were her manners. And how pleasant was her smile. He wished he could know her better and be friends with her. Then suddenly he remembered Red. He looked around for him. But the cook was nowhere to be found. He had disappeared completely.

Danny was worried. He had promised the Captain to look after Red. And Danny wanted to keep his promise. "Dear Lord Jesus," he prayed, "help me to find Red. And help me, too, to find Father."

2

IN FRONT of the post office, Danny stood perplexed, wondering how he should go about finding Red in San Francisco. At that moment the fire engine came clattering by, returning from the fire. Danny remembered that a crowd had rushed after the engine on its way to the fire. No doubt that was where Red had gone. If there was excitement anywhere, Red was sure to be in the middle of it!

Danny asked some of the people questions about the fire. It had been down near the wharf. Two stores had burned to the ground. Danny hurried off to the scene, confident that he would soon find Red.

There was still a crowd around the smoking ashes which were all that was left of the stores. The owners were telling the people that the stores would be rebuilt as soon as the ashes were cold. Fires were frequent in San Francisco, Danny learned. But no one seemed to worry about them. Whenever a structure burned down, a better one took its place.

It wasn't long until Danny caught a glimpse of a head of brick-colored hair and knew that he had found Red. But Red was hurrying in the opposite direction. Danny had to quicken his pace, weaving in and out of the crowd to catch up with him.

"Hello, Red!" he called. "Where are you going?"

Red turned around. "Oh, hello, Danny! I'm going to see a steamboat."

"I'd like to see it, too," Danny gasped. He was out of breath from hurrying. As soon as he got his breath he said, "What do you mean, running away like that, Red? I might have lost you!"

Red looked surprised. "I just ran after the fire engine." Then he stared at Danny, at his torn and muddy clothes. "What happened to you?"

"Oh, I ran after a kitten." Then Danny told him about Susanne and Tar Baby.

"I'm not the only one who ran away," Red said laughing.

"That's so," Danny had to admit.

"Then we're even!" Red said cheerfully.

"What's this steamboat we're going to see?" Danny asked.

"I heard some fellows talking about it," Red said excitedly. "It's a great little craft, they say."

Danny's eyes shone when he saw the boat. It was gleaming white with bright-yellow smokestacks. A flat-bottomed, side-wheeler, it bore the name *New World* painted in black.

"Pretty, ain't she?" asked a stranger.

Danny turned to look at the speaker. He was a man of middle age, well dressed.

"Yes, she is," Danny agreed. "Where does she go?"

"Up the Sacramento River."

"To Sacramento?"

"Yep! She goes to Sacramento. And crowded she'll be, too! That's the take-off place for the northern and southern mines."

Danny's heart was pounding. This, then, was the steamboat that Susanne had mentioned!

"When does she sail?" Red asked.

The man pulled out a heavy gold watch. "In about an hour."

"Could I get to Columbia from Sacramento?" Danny asked eagerly.

"Sure you can git thar. Take the coach to Sonora. That's the one you want."

Again the stranger consulted his watch, then said, "Either of you boys got a couple of four-bit pieces for a dollar?"

"Four-bit pieces? What are they?" Danny asked.

Red pulled out his wallet. "I got 'em, Mister." Danny saw him hand the man two fifty-cent pieces and the man gave Red a dollar in exchange.

"See you bin around," said the stranger.

"Sure," Red said, "I'm a seaman. I've been to the Sandwich Islands," he boasted.

"Do tell!" said the stranger admiringly. "Well, guess I'd better be on my way. If you boys want to sail on the *New World,* you'd better step up there and get your tickets."

Danny and Red hurried toward the wicket. An hour ago they had not known there was such a boat as the *New World*. Now it was their heart's desire to sail on her.

Danny was first in line. He bought his ticket. Then Red came behind him, asking for a ticket also. Red put his hand in his pocket, then gasped, "My wallet! It's gone! I've been robbed!"

Danny helped him search. One by one Red turned his pockets inside out. The wallet was gone.

"Buy a ticket or get out of line!" the crowd began to yell.

Hurriedly, Danny paid for Red's ticket.

"I can't go to Sacramento!" Red cried. "I got to find my wallet. Say, Danny, what about that stranger that talked to us? I mean the one that asked for two four-bit pieces. Maybe he's the one who robbed me!"

Danny felt shocked. "He didn't look like a robber, Red. He had a gold watch. He looked rich."

"Ha! Ha! He probably stole the watch, too!" said an old man near them. "Might as well give up, boys — never'll find the thief or the money either."

A shrill whistle sounded.

"That's the *New World*. Better hop on board, boys!" the old man advised.

"It's too bad, Red! But I have some money. And what's mine is yours, too," Danny said generously. He spoke quietly so that no one else would hear him.

"I feel sick all over," Red said.

"I got money enough to get to Columbia, Red. And Father will help you find a diggings. So cheer up. You'll have so much gold soon that you won't mind about losing your wallet!"

With these words, Danny managed to cheer Red.

The *New World* was crowded with passengers. Danny looked everywhere for Susanne. The boat had left San Francisco Bay, crossed San Pablo Bay, and was now passing, through the Straits of Carquinez into Suisun Bay before Danny found her. She was at the front of the steamer, leaning over the rail, looking into the churning waters whipped into white foam by the ship's paddles. Over her arm was the basket holding Tar Baby. With her was a young woman who looked so much like Susanne that Danny guessed at once she was her mother.

"Hello Susanne!" Danny said.

Susanne was pleased to see him. "Mother, this is Danny Winslow who captured my naughty little Tar Baby when he ran away."

Mrs. Edwards smiled at Danny. "I'm glad to meet you, Danny. Did you just arrive in California?"

"Just this morning, ma'am," Danny replied.

"We've been here a year," Susanne confided.

"Do you like it?" Danny asked.

"Yes, but it's a rough country. And we miss our church back home, don't we Mama?"

"Yes, indeed we do," Mrs. Edwards replied.

Danny was glad to know that Susanne and her mother were church-going people. It made him like them more than ever. He touched the carpet bag over his arm in which he carried all his belongings. "I have a Bible in here. I promised Mother to read a chapter every day."

"That is fine, Danny," Mrs. Edwards said. Susanne gave him a smile of warm approval.

"Are you traveling alone?" Mrs. Edwards asked.

"No, that's Red over there — Red Mitchell. He's my friend."

"Meow! Meow!" cried Tar Baby from the depths of the basket.

"Now be good, Tar Baby!" Susanne ordered the kitten. "I'm not going to open the lid. If I did, you'd be sure to jump out right into the water and be drowned."

When they parted for the night Mrs. Edwards said, "We shall be in Sacramento for a short time, Danny. If we can help you, let us know, won't you?"

"Indeed I will," Danny promised.

When the *New World* reached Sacramento in the early morning, there were crowds awaiting her arrival. They filled the galleries of the small hotels lining the waterfront.

It seemed to Danny that there must be at least a hundred stages lined up to meet the boat. And what noise and confusion filled the streets! Newsboys were screaming, "Another stage robbery! Wells Fargo offers three hundred dollars for capture of Virginia City express robber!"

Danny nearly collided with a two-wheeled, awkward looking cart or carriage which he learned was a Mexican *carreta.* It was drawn by a sleepy mule. Then they had to wait for a pack train with a long string of mules which passed along the street to the sharp cries of the muleteers' *"Hippah, mulah!"*

Danny and Red were jostled and pushed by the surging crowd. But Danny kept his eye on Red's brick-colored top and they managed to stay together.

They were both hungry and hurried to a hotel where meals were served. They entered a dark room, lighted dimly by candles. Eggs, they found, were to be had, but cost fifty cents each. So they contented themselves with beans and bread. The beans were half cooked and the bread was tough.

"I could do better myself!" Red snorted. "What they need here is a good cook!"

Danny grinned. "Maybe you could make money faster by cooking than by mining, Red."

Their breakfast finished, Dan looked for his money to pay the bill. He had felt his wallet in his pocket as they left the *New World*. But now it was gone. His face pale, his hands trembling, Danny searched his pockets. But his money was gone. They were "stuck"—no money to pay for their breakfast!

3

DANNY WAS really frightened when he realized that he and Red were now without money. And worse—he would have to explain to the hotel keeper that he and Red could not pay for their meal! What would they do? Well *he* could pray. And so quietly he asked God to help them.

The dining room was empty except for a man who sat in a far corner, writing figures in a book. "Guess I'd better tell him," Danny said to himself out loud. He approached the corner.

"Please, mister?" Danny began.

The man looked up, frowning. "Yes? What do you want? Oh, you want to pay your bill, eh?"

Danny swallowed hard. "I want to, sir. B-but I can't. My money's been stolen, sir."

The man stood up. He towered above Danny. "What's this?" he thundered. "Trying to cheat a hotel owner of his rightful due? I'll call the sheriff and have you put in jail."

"Oh, don't do that, sir," Danny pleaded. "We'll be glad to work to pay for our breakfast — and longer, too. We want to go to Columbia and we need money to get there."

"What can you do?"

"Red is a cook, sir."

The hotel man brightened. "A cook? Well, I do need a cook. But what can you do?"

"I can wait on tables, sir!"

The man smiled. "You're hired — both of you. Now get into the kitchen."

With Red as cook, the business of the hotel dining room picked up. For Red could cook well.

The hotel owner beamed at his new hired help. "You stay," he offered Red. "I pay magnificent wages. Two hundred dollars a month!"

But Red shook his head. He wanted to hunt gold. However, he would stay until he had enough money to outfit himself as a miner. And he and Danny had discovered that it would take considerable money. Miners' knives sold for thirty dollars. Candles were fifty cents each. Sugar was three dollars a pound.

And while Red cooked and dreamed of the rich vein of gold he would some day discover, Danny ran back and forth from the kitchen to the dining room, waiting on customers. By listening to the conversation around him, Danny began to be familiar with the ways of the new West. He heard the name Wells Fargo frequently. He grew to know the stage-coach drivers by name. He stood in awe of the fearless shotgun messengers sent by Wells Fargo to guard the treasure in the stout, green iron-bound boxes. He heard frequently of robberies and "hold-ups," for the treasure box which rode at the feet of the driver was the object sought by all the bandits of the West.

One morning two men entered the dining room. Danny hurried to wait on them. One wore high and handsome lace boots and a cream-colored, broad-brimmed hat. The other wore dark clothes. The man in the fancy dress was Charlie, a stagecoach driver.

They were talking excitedly and Danny asked, "Another robbery, sir?"

Charlie nodded. "A bad one this time, Danny. Three robbers made off with one hundred thousand dollars in gold dust."

Danny's eyes grew wide. "One hundred thousand dollars!" It was a fabulous sum!

"A man gets on the stage," Charlie was saying to his companion, the man in the dark suit. "He's dressed like a miner. But he's not a miner. His eye is on that Wells Fargo treasure box. He knows it's loaded. How he knows, I cannot say. But he knows."

"Was anyone with him?" Charlie's friend asked.

"No, the driver, Jim, is alone. No messenger rides with him. Jim stops for a change of horses. The passenger he gets off. He goes to the dining room.

"Driver Jim says, 'Ain't you comin'?'

"The man says, 'No — waiting fer the next one.'

"Driver Jim goes on. He's got new passengers. And all is peaceful and quiet, but not for long! You know where that road winds along over the mountains thar, between Milton and Sonora? Well, Jim was driving along when out of the bushes pops three men, armed to the hilt. 'Halt!' they orders. So Jim halts.

" 'Hand down that box!' they says.

" 'Can't,' Jim says. 'It's bolted to the floor.'

" 'Git down then. Git the passengers out.' So Jim gits down. And the passengers, they gits down, too. Then the robbers tell Jim to unhitch his hosses. So Jim does it. Then the robbers go to work on the box. They rip it loose with their hatchet. Then they go off through the woods. Driver

Jim hitches up his team. The passengers get back in the stage. Jim makes for Sonora and reports the robbery."

The man in the black suit shook his head. "Wells Fargo has posted eight hundreds dollars as reward for capture of the bandits."

Charlie nodded. "Hope they git them."

"What would you do, Charlie, if a bit of cold steel were pointed your way and a voice said, 'Hand down the treasure box or I'll shoot to kill'?"

"They wouldn't get that box if I was alive!" Charlie said.

The man in the dark suit shook his head. "Look at that Dry Creek Gulch hold-up, Charlie! The driver and Wells Fargo's messenger put up a fight and what happened? One passenger was killed, two were wounded, and the driver had a bullet in his arm. No, siree, *I'd* say, 'Take the box.' "

That night Danny told Red all about the robbery and the eight hundred dollars in reward offered by Wells Fargo for the capture of the robbers. But Red hardly heard. He was counting his money and he discovered that he had enough for his outfit.

"Tomorrow we leave for Columbia!" Red shouted proudly.

Danny was so excited he could hardly sleep. Tomorrow perhaps he would see Father. Danny had only one regret on leaving Sacramento. He had not seen Susanne again.

The hotel owner wept when they left. "The country is full of miners," he said. "But good cooks are few. Stay and I'll double your wages."

Red shook his head. He had come to find gold.

At dawn Danny and Red started out. The drivers were calling their routes with gusto.

"All aboard!" shouted Charlie. "Ione Valley, Jackson, Mokelumne Hill, Chilean Gulch, Yankee Camp, Angel's

Camp, Half-Oz Gulch, Tuttletown, Shaw's Flat, Columbia, and Sonora!"

Danny was delighted to find that their driver would be Charlie. The coach seemed already full but Charlie said, "Squeeze in. You boys is skinny."

So Danny and Red squeezed in. It was dark within the coach and Danny could not see the faces of the other passengers.

"All aboard!" Charlie shouted. There was a crack of a long whip, a shout, "Git along, thar!" and the wheels began to hum. The coach leaped forward.

Crack! Crack! went the whip. The hoofs of the four horses thumped and clattered on the hard, dry road. The passengers bounced up and down on the seats. They were knocked to the right and to the left, jostling one another.

Soon it began to be light and Danny could see the other passengers. There were Chinese with long pigtails hanging down their backs. There was a fat Negro lady. There was an old lady with a bird cage on her lap. There were rough miners and well-dressed merchants.

The old lady with the bird cage nudged Danny. "Where you going, young man?"

"To Columbia," Danny said.

"I'm going to Sonora and I hopes I git thar. What with that there treasure box with Wells Fargo gold and these bandits shootin' up everybody on the way, we might git to heaven instead."

Danny swallowed. "Well, heaven's a nice place."

"I allows that," said the old lady. "But I'm not in a hurry to git thar."

"How do you know that there's such a place as heaven?" Red asked, joining the conversation.

"Because the Bible says so," Danny answered.

"Supposing you didn't lead the right kind of life? How can you know if you'll get there or not?" Red asked. "Not that I'm expecting to leave this world right now," he added.

"If you believe that the Lord Jesus died on the cross for your sins and if you accept Him as your Saviour, then you can be sure of getting to heaven."

Red didn't answer. He just stared out the window with a far-away look on his face.

"That's right smartly spoken, young man!" said the little old lady. "I reckon you'll be a preacher when you grow up."

"I don't know about that," Danny answered, "but I'm a Christian and that's one thing I'm sure about."

Crack! went the long whip. The coach lurched and came dangerously near toppling over and tumbling down the canyon.

"Goodness!" the old lady groaned. "Will we ever git there alive?"

4

CRACK! "Git along thar!" shouted Charlie, snapping the whip. The horses plunged forward. Faster and faster the coach raced along. Danny was flung first against one passenger, then another. Sometimes he bounced so high his head hit the roof. The old lady clung to her bird cage, shouting, "Goodness! My poor old bones!" The Chinese squealed and their long pigtails whipped across the faces of their fellow passengers.

"Watch out for that turn ahead!" someone shouted.

The coach lurched. Then when the curve was passed, it dashed on. Now and then Charlie stopped for a change of horses. But it was only a matter of minutes until they were on the road again.

When a wayside hotel came into view, the passengers were allowed to alight, stretch their limbs and partake of a lunch of beans and bread pudding. Then they were again on their way.

It was late afternoon on a narrow mountain road when a sharp voice sounded almost in Danny's ear. "Throw down that treasure box, or I shoot to kill!"

Charlie abruptly drew rein. Danny felt his spine tingle. He looked at Red. Red's mouth was open and his eyes were wide with fright.

"Goodness, what's up now?" screamed the old lady with the bird cage. "It must be them highway robbers!"

"I wouldn't pull in if you was alone," said Charlie in a cool voice, "but with your two pals comin' around that tree yonder—"

The robber turned in surprise. In that moment Charlie cracked his long whip, knocking the gun from the bandit's hand.

"Gid-up thar!" shouted Charlie. The wheels of the coach began to turn faster and faster. Cracking and snapping his whip and yelling like a wild Indian, Charlie urged the horses forward. The coach plunged along the narrow road, the passengers tossed together like so many sticks.

"Those three bandits will be after us sure!" the old lady said in between her moans.

Charlie chuckled. "They was only one bandit lady! 'Twas a trick and it worked."

How glad Danny and Red were that they were safe! Danny kept hoping and praying that they would get to Columbia soon. But Columbia was farther than Danny thought. It was dark when the coach reached the Fourth Crossing. There they were to stay for the night.

Danny was glad to turn in even though his bed was only a narrow straw mattress. The pillow was without a case, and there was only one blanket for covering. The beds were bunks along the wall. Before he got into bed, Danny knelt down to pray.

They were awakened before dawn. It was not yet light when the coach went clattering on its way. Altaville, Angel's Camp, Carson Hill, Melones were soon safely past. The coach rattled on into Tuttletown. Here the Negro lady alighted. All the others in the coach except Red and Danny were bound for Sonora.

It was noon when the coach reached Columbia. Danny's heart pounded strangely as he and Red said good-by to Charlie and the other passengers. Soon, Danny was sure, he would see Father.

Miners, merchants, adventurers, and gamblers passed in and out of the adobe, iron-doored structures along the single business street of the town. Danny had no difficulty finding the Wells Fargo office. It was a red brick building with an iron balcony. Above the balcony were the words, "Wells Fargo & Co." and below the balcony in large letters was the word "Express."

Danny clutched the letter in his pocket. Now to find Father.

The office was crowded. Danny patiently awaited his turn. When the manager asked, "What can I do for you?" Danny drew Father's letter from his pocket.

"I'm Danny Winslow and my father said in case he didn't meet me in San Francisco, I was to ask for him here. He said to show you this letter."

The Wells Fargo agent took the letter, read it quickly, then said, "Just a minute, Danny, till I consult my records and refresh my memory." The agent soon returned saying that he remembered Danny's father but it had been some time since he had seen him. "Your father has a partner, Duke Wells. Duke has been around. He can tell you where to find your father."

The agent showed Danny a rough map of the gold mining region and pointed out Dry Creek where he said Danny's father and Duke Wells had their diggings. After looking at the map carefully, Danny said that he and Red could find Dry Creek.

As they came out of the office, they saw a man on horseback preaching to a crowd who had gathered around him. The man had a Bible in his hand and was saying, "All the stores in this town are open on the Lord's Day except one. Have you all forgotten God? You look for treasure and when you have it you are afraid that thieves will steal it. Lay up for yourselves treasures in heaven where thieves cannot steal."

When the preacher finished, he jumped down from his horse and the people came and talked to him. Danny went too, and shook hands with the preacher whose name was Peter Wing. Danny told him his name and where he was from. He told him he had come to find his father who was somewhere along Dry Creek.

"I'm traveling that way tomorrow," the preacher said kindly. "Like to go along?"

"Sure!" replied Danny. "And will it be all right for my friend Red to come along, too?"

"Of course," answered Peter Wing.

Danny was delighted. To have someone to go with who knew the way would make finding Father much quicker and easier.

The next morning the preacher, Danny, and Red started out for Dry Creek. Even in early morning the day promised to be hot. There were many miners traveling back and forth, many on foot. They all carried the familiar pan, pick, and shovel, and wore broad-brimmed hats and boots with the trouser legs laced inside of them. Some were singing. Some looked happy. But some looked discouraged and down-hearted.

The preacher often stopped to talk to the miners and to give them the Word of God. Danny and Red rested. Often the preacher walked beside his horse and let Danny or Red ride.

They talked of the big robbery in which the robbers had got away with one hundred thousand dollars in gold dust.

"I feel sorry for those miners that lost their money in

that holdup," Danny said to Peter Wing. "They worked so hard to dig their gold."

"The miners didn't lose it, Danny. Wells Fargo makes it up to them, every penny. It's Wells Fargo that loses."

"Oh, no wonder Father said that Wells Fargo is the miner's best friend!"

"They have proved themselves worthy of trust, Danny. That is sure. It is a wonderful thing to have a good name, to be worthy of trust. The Bible says, 'A good name is rather to be chosen than great riches.' You read the Bible, don't you, Danny? And do you believe what it says?"

"Oh, yes!" answered Danny. "And I believe in the Lord Jesus, too!"

"That's fine!" said Peter Wing as they went on their way.

That night they stayed at a miner's camp. Early in the morning they were on their way again.

At last they reached Dry Creek. Danny grew more and more excited. It might be only a matter of minutes until he should see Father. What a big hug he would give him! How wonderful to see his dear father once again!

The preacher began asking for the Winslow-Wells diggings. One miner said, "I haven't seen Winslow for a long time. But Wells is there." He stopped his work and pointed out the exact place.

Danny's heart sank. But hadn't the Wells Fargo man said that Mr. Wells would be able to help him find his father?

"Are you Duke Wells?" the preacher asked of a man who was busy with his pick.

"That's who I am," the man responded. But he did not seem very friendly.

"I'm a preacher. Peter Wing is the name. And this is Red Mitchell. And this is Danny Winslow."

At the name Winslow, Duke Wells looked sharply at Danny.

"They told me you were Father's partner," Danny said. "I've come to find Father. They said you could tell me where he is."

For a moment Duke Wells looked as if he had seen a ghost. Then he shook his head. "I ain't seen him for a long time."

"Aren't you his partner?" Danny asked.

"Naw. I bought him out. This is my digging."

"Did he say where he was going?" Danny asked.

Duke Wells hesitated, then said, "He was headin' for the Sierras last time I seen him."

"I've got to find him," Danny cried. "I'll never give up till I do."

Duke Wells looked at him. "I've an idea where he might be," he said. "I'd go along with you if I didn't have to watch my diggings."

"How long will it take?" the preacher asked.

"Two or three days," Duke Wells responded.

"I'll watch your diggings, then," the preacher said. "Red you go with Danny and help him find his father. You can take my horse with you."

Danny was glad to have help in finding Father. But there was something about Duke Wells that he didn't like. Could he be trusted?

5

LEAVING THE brush-covered, grassy hills, where great live oaks dotted the landscape, Duke Wells, Red and Danny soon came to the edge of the forests. Giant pines, firs, and cedars formed a woodland of great beauty. Here there were only single trails to follow. Beyond the forests were huge granite mountain ranges, the great giant peaks of the Sierras.

The country abounded in rivers, streams, and lakes.

Here and there miners panned for gold, hurrying to secure all that they could before the winter season forced them to abandon their diggings.

At length the three reached a steep grade where a trail, if there was one, was hidden in the thick undergrowth.

"Reckon we'd better tie the preacher's horse here," Duke Wells said. " 'Tain't far to the cabin where we'll have to spend the night."

But it seemed far to Danny. Sometimes he thought that they must be going around in circles. He had noticed a tree badly scarred as if a fire had been built near it. It was a ragged cedar. And it seemed to Danny that he saw the tree again and again. But no doubt there were many ragged cedars in the forest which had had fires built close to them. Duke Wells appeared confident. Surely he knew the way.

A full moon helped to illumine their way.

"There it is," Duke Wells said.

"Is Father here?" Danny asked.

"No. We will sleep here and then go on, higher in the Sierras."

The cabin had a dirt floor, rough wooden windows and a heavy door. At one end was a small loft.

"You and Red sleep in the loft," Duke Wells said. "There's grizzly bears in these mountains. Snakes, too. I'll sleep down here, case there's any danger."

Danny decided that Duke Wells must be a brave man after all. Probably he had been mistaken about him. Yes, Duke Wells must be all right.

But Danny did not have much time to think. He was exhausted from his long day of travel. Red was too and soon they were both sound asleep. Though they had only a hard board for a bed and their arms for pillows and no covering over them, they slept soundly.

Suddenly Danny was awakened by loud voices in rough dispute. Red, too, sat up. They could see a patch of moonlight on the wall and knew that a door or window was open. Cautiously they crept to the edge of the loft and peered down.

Below them in a patch of moonlight three men sat in cross-legged fashion. Before them was a heavy, iron-bound box with the lid open. Danny stared. He noticed that Duke Wells was not one of the men. Where was Duke and what had happened to him?

" 'Tain't safe to carry this here treasure!" one of the men was saying. "Like as not the sheriff and his posse's headed this way. Let's bury it. That's what I say."

Danny's eyes popped as he saw the heavy bags lifted from the box — the green treasure box of Wells Fargo! One hundred thousand dollars in gold dust!

"I'm aiming to quit this business," one of the men growled. "Getting too dangerous. I want my share now. I want to get out of this country."

"If you want to get out alive, you'd best listen to reason, Tex. 'Tain't healthy to be caught with Wells Fargo loot."

"No," said the third man. "Bury it. That's what I say. When Wells Fargo forgits, we kin come back and git it. That's what I say."

"Wells Fargo never forgits, that's the trouble!"

"Well, the excitement's sure to die down. Then's when to git off with this gold dust."

"Yeah. It's two to one, Tex. You jest listen to reason."

"All right then. Jest what you say."

The bags of gold dust were put back in the green treasure chest. Taking up the chest, the men left the cabin.

Danny nudged Red. "I'm going to see where they put it, Red," he whispered.

"Look out, Danny," Red cautioned. "The moon is bright as can be. How can you hide in this light? If you go out that door, they'll see you sure."

"I'll climb out that back window. The trees hide it there."

Cautiously Danny crept down the ladder. Keeping close to the walls, he was careful not to get in the stream of light. He stopped and listened. The men were in the front of the cabin. He could hear their voices. Cautiously he moved to a window. The bars creaked as he slid them back. He waited breathlessly. But the men continued their work. Danny climbed out the window. Sliding along the walls of the cabin, he moved cautiously from the back to the side, keeping under the shadow of the trees. At the edge of the cabin he could see the men. They were about thirty feet from the cabin in an open space between two tall pines. They placed the box in a hole as he watched, then replaced the dirt over it and packed the surface down.

Suddenly in the still night there came the sound of a piercing scream, then the sound of horses' hoofs. Terrified, Danny clung to the side of the cabin. The men looked this way and that, trying to make up their minds which way to run. Danny closed his eyes and prayed. If they came his way, he would be gone for sure.

But the men turned and fled in the opposite direction, throwing their shovels in the thicket at the edge of the clearing and disappearing into the forest.

Danny ran back into the cabin. Red was already climbing down the ladder.

"Did you hear that scream, Red?"

"I sure did!"

"I wonder what happened to Duke Wells?" Danny asked. "Do you suppose he is in with these robbers?"

"I don't know, Danny. But one thing I do know. I'd sure like to get down from this mountain."

"We'll have to tell the sheriff about the treasure box, Red. Let's go back to where Duke tied the preacher's horse."

"Maybe we'd better take the gold with us," Red said. "The robbers might come back and dig it up before we get back."

"Let's us dig it up, Red. We'll bury it behind the cabin. I saw where they threw their shovels."

"Hope no one sees us!" Red said as he hurriedly shoved the earth away from the buried box.

They were astonished at its weight. "We could never carry this with us," Danny said.

Red agreed. Carrying the heavy box together, they dug a place behind the cabin and buried it under a pine tree. This work finished, they started down the mountain.

They had gone only a short way when Danny pointed. "Look, Red. The preacher's horse was tied here."

There was a wide place where the grass was trampled down. Red examined the spot. "It looks like it right enough. But last night it seemed much farther away. It couldn't be as close as this."

Danny frowned. "But this is it, Red! It's a funny thing but last night I was sure we were going round and round. Do you suppose Duke Wells did it on purpose?"

"Why'd he want to do something like that?"

Danny shrugged. "Don't know, I'm sure. But see, here's that ragged cedar with the burned spot. It's the only one we've seen. Last night we must have passed it a dozen times."

Red shook his head. "It looks like the spot but it can't be, 'cause the horse's not here. That's evidence, isn't it?"

"I still think that it's the spot. Duke Wells and the horse are both gone."

Gradually the dawn began to lighten the sky. The sun came up. They had been walking about an hour when Danny stopped suddenly. "I think we've taken the wrong trail, Red. We're getting deeper into the forest."

"I was thinking that too, Danny. What will we do if we get lost? We could die in these mountains and no one would find us. I'm hungry, aren't you?"

"Yes, I am," Danny admitted. "Say, Red. Let's have a prayer right here, shall we?"

"I don't know how to pray," Red admitted.

"I'll pray then," Danny said. They both knelt and bowed their heads. "Dear Father in heaven," Danny prayed, "please show us the way to go. Thou knowest the way. Help us to find it. In Jesus' name, Amen."

When they stood up, Red said, "I wish I could pray."

"You can, Red, if you're a Christian."

"I'd like to be, Danny. What'll I do?"

"Do you believe that the Lord Jesus died on the cross for you?"

"Why — yes," Red said, not being sure of himself.

"Well, if you really believe with your heart that He's your Saviour, you ought to know how to pray. And you'll also believe that God raised Him from the dead and that He is alive now. Do you see?"

"Yes," Red said, bowing his head reverently. "I really believe all that. But I certainly haven't lived the way I should and the way I learned to live when I went to Sunday school."

"The Lord Jesus can save you from your sins and give you eternal life if you will believe. And if you do He can make you sure of salvation — that's what Mother used to tell me."

"Yes," Red answered, "I know that, too. I really believe, Danny."

"Then you're a Christian and you can pray. Why don't you now, Red, just thank God for being so good to you and saving you?"

Red bowed his head. "Thank Thee, Lord, for saving me." Then he smiled. "You know, Danny, I'm not afraid now! I'm *sure* the Lord will show us the way down from this mountain."

6 IT WASN'T long until Danny and Red once more reached the place where the grass was crushed down and where Danny was sure the preacher's horse had been left.

Danny grinned. "You know, Red, when you find you've been going in the wrong way, the thing to do is to turn around and go in the opposite way? Then you're *sure* to go in the right direction!"

Taking a new trail, they had not gone far before they heard faint cries for help. They stopped, listening carefully.

"I think it comes from the canyon down there," Red said.

"Hello! Hello!" Danny called.

"Hello! Help! Help!" came back a cry.

Danny and Red began to descend into the canyon. "Where are you?" Danny called.

"Here! Here!"

The voice didn't sound far away. Danny spotted what looked like a dark bundle of rags. "Over there, Red. That looks like it might be someone."

The boys hurried forward. They soon discovered a man sitting with his knees drawn up to his chin. As the boys came closer they saw that the man was Duke Wells.

When Duke saw them, he cried out in terror, "Don't kill me! Don't kill me!"

Danny and Red looked at one another. "He must be out of his head!" Danny said. "He doesn't recognize us."

"Don't be afraid, Mr. Wells," Danny said. "It's Red and I. We've come to help you."

Duke Wells began to whimper. His dark beady eyes still regarded them with suspicion. He still seemed dazed.

"What happened to you, Mr. Wells? How do you happen to be so far away from the cabin?" Danny didn't find it easy to call him Duke.

"It was that preacher's horse that done it," Mr. Wells groaned. "He tossed me off him like I was a sack of flour."

"So you were the one who screamed!" Danny said. "Are you hurt much?"

"No — just twisted my foot and got a bump on my head — sorta knocked me out, I guess."

"What were you doing on the preacher's horse?" demanded Red. "Running away from us? Leaving us alone on the mountain to get lost or to starve to death?"

"Oh, my leg! My leg!" Mr. Wells moaned, rubbing his left foot.

"Maybe he was running away from the robbers," Danny whispered to Red.

"Robbers? What robbers?" Mr. Wells demanded—he'd heard Danny.

"Didn't you see the robbers, Mr. Wells? There were three of them. They were the robbers that held up the Milton to Sonora stage and made off with the Wells Fargo green treasure box. They had a hundred thousand dollars in gold dust, they say. And there's eight hundred dollars reward for capture of the robbers."

Duke sat up. "You — *you* saw the robbers? And the gold?"

"Yep!" Danny said. "They buried it up there and we're on our way to tell the sheriff."

"Don't do that, boys!" Mr. Wells said pleadingly. He tried to get to his feet but couldn't make it. So he leaned toward them, his eyes glittering. "A hundred thousand dollars! Why you might dig for years and not find that much gold. Listen, boys. I'll tell you what we'll do. We'll be partners in this. Let's dig up that treasure and divide it among us."

Danny stared at Mr. Wells. He could hardly believe his ears. Mr. Wells must indeed be out of his head. "No — that wouldn't be honest! We *couldn't* do that!"

"Who's to know?" Mr. Wells demanded, his head seeming to clear. "No one will see us."

"God will see us," Danny answered. "God says, 'Thou shalt not steal.' "

Mr. Wells turned away. His beady eyes grew cunning. "Tell me where the gold is and I'll tell you where to find your father."

"I can't tell you where the gold is," Danny said. "But you will tell me where my father is, won't you? You wouldn't be so cruel as not to tell me, would you?"

"Wouldn't I?" Duke asked. "You'll *never* find your father unless you tell me where the gold is buried!"

Red spoke up. "If Mr. Wells won't tell you where your father is, Danny, we can just go off and leave him. The bears or the snakes or something will get him sure."

Danny shook his head. "We couldn't do that, Red."

"Why not?"

" 'Cause we're Christians and as Christians we have to do good even to those who hate us."

"But that doesn't make sense," Red argued. "If a fellow hits me, I want to hit him back. Give him just as good as he gives me."

Danny nodded. "I know, that's what we feel like doing. But the Lord Jesus didn't do that. We're supposed to be like Him as much as we can. We are to be kind and to treat everyone just as we want them to treat us. If I was injured like Duke — Mr. Wells — here I'd want someone to help me and I wouldn't want them to go off and leave me to the bears and the snakes."

Duke Wells was looking at Danny and Red in astonishment as he listened to this conversation. But Red and Danny were so absorbed in their conversation that they weren't even noticing him.

Red was saying, "There's more to being a Christian than I thought. Maybe I can't be a Christian after all."

"Of course you can, Red! Whenever you don't feel like a Christian, just pray about it. Just tell the Lord Jesus that you don't feel like much of a Christian and ask Him to make you feel like one. He will do it, Red."

"Maybe I'd better do it right now," Red said. He bowed his head, then prayed, "Dear Lord Jesus, I sure seem to hate Mr. Wells and I know that You don't like me to hate anyone. So, dear Lord, please make me not hate him. Make me kind to him, dear Lord, 'cause I guess You died for him as well as for me."

When Red looked up, he grinned at Mr. Wells saying, "I do feel better about you now, Mr. Wells. C'mon, Danny, let's help him."

With the aid of both boys, Mr. Wells got to his feet. To his surprise he found he could step on his foot. "Guess I didn't break any bones, after all," he said. But his foot was so badly swollen that the boys had to cut his boot off. Danny took off his own shirt, tore it in strips and bound Mr. Wells' swollen foot. With their hands the boys made a seat to carry Mr. Wells up from the canyon. Fortunately, he was a slight man. He put his arms around the boys' necks. Slowly the three climbed back onto the road.

Even though Mr. Wells was not too heavy, it was hard for the boys to carry him down the mountain. It seemed to them that they were making very little progress. They stopped to rest quite often.

Suddenly Danny shouted, "Look, Red, there's the preacher's horse!" Red and Mr. Wells both looked. Surely enough, there was the preacher's horse a short ways ahead of them, peacefully eating grass.

Depositing Mr. Wells by the side of the road, the boys ran to the horse. He seemed glad to see them and waved his head and neighed. Danny led him to where Mr. Wells was sitting. Carefully, they hoisted Duke on his back and again started down the mountain. But they had not gone far until Mr. Wells gave a loud shout, "Look out, boys!" He dug his heels into the side of the horse, turned him about, and started racing up the mountain. The horse went like fury.

Danny and Red stared after him in astonishment.

"He's after the gold," Red cried. "Let's follow him."

Danny hesitated. If they went after Duke Wells it would delay getting the sheriff. And if the robbers came back and found them at the cabin, what could they do? The robbers had guns while they were unarmed. And how could Mr. Wells dig for the treasure when he could hardly stand on his feet? Besides, it would take him time to find the buried treasure. No, it would be better to get the news to the sheriff and Wells Fargo as quickly as they could.

"We're almost out of the mountains now, Red. Let's get the sheriff and his posse."

Soon the boys were passing solitary miners and groups of miners. But they said nothing of the buried treasure. After their experience with Mr. Wells, they decided they must be careful about telling of their discovery.

But before they reached the foothills, night had fallen. Tired and hungry, they lay down exhausted on the dry grass. The wind whispered through the trees and wild rabbits stirred the brush. But the two slept on.

At dawn Danny awoke. He prayed that the Lord would help them find the sheriff before Duke Wells discovered the hiding place of the green treasure box.

"We have to be on our way, Red," Danny said, as he woke Red.

Would they be in time to save the Wells Fargo treasure? Danny wondered about this as they again started down the trail.

7

DANNY AND Red were again in the foothills of the Sierras. Hungry and tired, they at last reached Dry Creek where the preacher was anxiously waiting for them.

When Peter Wing saw how exhausted Danny and Red

were he insisted that they rest themselves and have something to eat. But Danny and Red were so full of their news they could not wait to tell it. And so they told the whole story.

The preacher nodded. "I've been inquiring about that fellow Duke Wells and I didn't like what I heard. I was about to get the sheriff to take a little trip with me to find you fellows. But now you're here we'll all go after him together — that is, as soon as you finish your meal."

As the two ate, they gave the preacher further details of their experiences. "Duke Wells knows where my father is but he said he wouldn't tell me unless I let him know where the gold is buried," Danny said.

"Don't you worry about that!" the preacher reassured Danny. "We'll get Duke Wells to tell."

"Yes, if we can find him," Danny said. "And what about your fine horse?"

"And if he doesn't find the gold first and get away with it," Red added.

"I've been getting acquainted with some of the neighbors," the preacher nodded toward other prospectors near. "They're nice boys and I think I can round up a horse for each of us. And don't worry about my horse."

Before long the three were riding down to Columbia in search of the sheriff. He was quickly found and as soon as he heard Danny's news, rounded up his men. Neither, Danny, nor Red, nor the preacher wanted to miss any of the excitement so they rode along too.

"The old mountain begins to look mighty familiar," Danny said as they again reached the forest region.

"Look, Mr. Wing," Danny cried, drawing his horse close to the preacher's. "There's your horse that Duke Wells rode off with. He must be near somewhere."

"Couldn't get far with that game leg," Red added.

Although darkness had fallen, the moon shone full on the cabin in the clearing. And in the moonlight the solitary figure of a man was revealed. He was digging in the exact spot where the robbers had buried the gold.

The man must have heard their approach. For he looked up and the shovel fell from his hands. Danny saw that the man was Tex. He had come back to dig up the treasure!

Tex started to draw his gun.

"Hands up!" the sheriff called.

"Looking for something?" the sheriff asked as Tex raised both arms.

"Just prospectin' for a little gold," Tex replied.

The sheriff grinned. "Won't find it in that spot, partner! There's been prospectors here before you."

"Double-crossed," Tex groaned. "The hounds double-crossed me."

"Looks to me like the pot calling the kettle black," the sheriff answered as his men took Tex into custody. The sheriff turned to Danny. "Say, boy, where'd you bury that green treasure box?"

Danny led the way to the rear of the cabin and showed the sheriff the place where he and Red had buried the Wells Fargo treasure box. The sheriff started digging. Danny breathed a sigh of relief as the spade hit the hard wood of the chest. The green box was drawn up and opened. The gold dust was safe.

"There will be a nice little reward waiting for you boys!" the sheriff said.

"A reward is nice," Danny replied, "but what I want most is to find my father."

"Of course you do," the sheriff answered heartily. "Well, I'll tell you what we'll do. My boys and I will ride down with this gold and put it safe in the hands of Wells Fargo. And we'll put this Tex fellow safe in jail. Then we'll come along back and go on up in the Sierra country to look for your father. A couple of my boys will wait here with you. They've plenty of grub."

"Yeh, but who will cook it?" asked one of the men.

"Red can cook," Danny said.

"Just show me the food," Red agreed.

They were singing and having a good time when a shadowy figure appeared near the cabin. The sheriff's men jumped to their feet and drew their guns. But the man held up both hands, crying, "Don't shoot. I'm harmless. Just smelled that good food and wanted some."

Danny and Red stared at the man in astonishment. It was Duke Wells.

"What happened to you, Duke?" Danny cried.

Duke rubbed his arms ruefully. "That preacher's horse threw me again."

"It's a knowing horse!" the preacher said proudly.

"Give me some of that good venison," Duke Wells pleaded. "I'm starved to death."

"First tell me where my father is," Danny insisted.

"I'll tell you anything to get some food," Duke Wells agreed. "Last time I saw your father, Danny, he was in a cabin about three miles on up. Had a fever and I had to leave him. Had to get back to our digging."

"My father was sick and you left him?" Danny cried. "You're a fine partner!"

"Well, if I didn't someone would steal our diggings," Duke replied.

Danny wanted to go immediately to find his father, so the men agreed.

As Duke Wells couldn't walk any further, he was given a horse. Guarded by the sheriff's men, he led the way. At last a cabin came into view. When the men pushed open the door, Danny gasped. There was his father with a gun in his hand and before him were the other two robbers who had been with Tex in the Wells Fargo hold-up.

"Just holding these men for the sheriff," Mr. Winslow said as he saw the sheriff's men.

"Father!" Danny cried.

Then Father whirled around. "Danny!" was all he could say.

Danny hugged Father and Father hugged him. Danny could scarcely believe his eyes.

"How did you get here, Danny?"

"Duke Wells showed us the way."

"Duke Wells? Then I'll forgive him for running off and leaving me when I was ill with a fever."

Duke Wells came forward. "I've been a wicked man, Mr. Winslow. I confess it. I stole your horse and left you to die of fever. And I brought your boy and this other lad up the mountain and deserted them. When they found me in the canyon with an injured foot, they helped me out. But again I turned against them, seeking to find and to keep the Wells Fargo treasure. But that preacher's horse dumped me a second time and I started to do some thinking. I kept remembering what the boys said about being Christians. I thought I'd like to try it if it wasn't too late. Do you think God could forgive such a great sinner as I am?"

"Of course He will," Father said. "If we confess our sins, He is faithful and just to forgive us our sins and to cleanse us from all unrighteousness."

"That's right, Mr. Winslow," said the preacher. "I think Duke Wells is going to be a new man and a different man from now on."

"Before we go," Danny said, "I'd like to say thanks to the Lord Jesus for helping me find Father and for being so good to us all."

"That's a fine idea," the preacher said. "Let's all bow our heads and our hearts in prayer."

The sheriff's men with their prisoners, Danny and Father, Red, the preacher and Duke Wells started down the mountain. They had not gone far until they met the sheriff. With him was Mr. Edwards of the Wells Fargo and Company.

"There will be a nice reward for you boys," Mr. Edwards said, "and for Mr. Winslow, too, for capturing the other two robbers."

Danny's father smiled. "Having my boy is my reward."

"Father," Danny cried, "will you help Red find a digging? He wants to look for gold."

"Changed my mind," Red said, "think I'll go back to Sacramento and get that job as a cook with that double pay. Nothing like a regular income."

"You're wise there, Red," Mr. Edwards said. "This gold rush won't last forever. It's tapering off right now."

"I've been thinking the same thing," Father said.

"Fine," Mr. Edwards returned. "Could I persuade you to come with Wells Fargo?"

"I think you could," Father answered.

Danny looked at Mr. Edwards. "Say, you don't happen to be Susanne's father, do you?"

"I certainly do. And I've orders to bring you down to see her. Susanne will never forget the boy who saved Tar Baby."

"It will be nice to see Tar Baby again," Danny said.

Mr. Edwards laughed heartily. "How about Susanne, Danny? Won't you be glad to see her again?"

Danny grinned. "Sure. It will be nice to see Mrs. Edwards, Susanne and Tar Baby."

Danny decided that when he reached Columbia he would write two letters, one to Mother and one to Captain Bartholomew telling them that Father had been found and was safe. But Danny couldn't decide whether he'd work for Wells Fargo when he grew up or whether he'd be a preacher.

The Chinese Jinx

1 JIM ROGERS dug his hands into the pockets of his trousers. Then he thrust them into his coat pockets. The pockets were all empty. Only yesterday he had had his pay as cabin boy on the *Marietta* in his pockets. But last night as he slept on the floor of the lodging house on Montgomery Street he had been robbed. And when he awoke in the morning, his pockets were empty. A few coins had escaped because they happened to be in his trousers pocket. But what were a few paltry coins? With a shrug of the shoulders he walked along the street.

There was no use to return to the *Marietta* anchored in San Francisco Bay, for the *Marietta* had been abandoned by the captain and his crew, all of whom had gone off to the "diggings" to find gold. The crew had scattered, each man making his own way to the gold fields. Captain Weatherbee might still be in San Francisco but the chance of finding him in the narrow, crowded streets of this bustling town was not great.

Still, Captain Weatherbee was the only person Jim knew and so Jim set out to find him.

"Good thing for me," Jim muttered to himself, "that I paid for my night's lodging in advance! If I hadn't, that hatchet-faced proprietor might have thrown me in prison when I couldn't pay."

Jim looked wistfully through the open doors of the restaurants he passed. The smell of frying bacon and steaming coffee made him tighten his belt and walk quickly past. How hungry he was!

But no one would imagine that he would be hungry. No one would take him to be a young man. His full sixteen years deceived people. They always looked at his short height and young face and laughed. They always twitted him when he told them his age.

But he was a man for all people thought! And he had a grown man's appetite, too. Yes, and he could do a man's work — any day!

He let a sigh escape his lips. He hurried past the open markets and the busy restaurants. Then just as the crowds began to thin out somewhat, Jim stopped to look around. One end of Montgomery Street ended at a high hill, called Telegraph Hill, but in the opposite direction the street was fairly level. Jim walked along, looking eagerly this way and that for Captain Weatherbee's tall figure. But the Captain was nowhere to be seen. No doubt, he, too, had already gone off to the diggings.

Jim felt forlorn. He was homeless and all but penniless in a strange city. It was a city where there were wicked men, men who wouldn't hesitate for a moment to rob a youth of all his earnings. They were men who would, doubtless, spend the money on drink.

Jim thought of his widowed mother and wished he had stayed at home in Baltimore. All his dreams of finding gold were gone, for how could he get to the gold country without money for steamship or coach fare and without money to buy the tools and provisions he would need to pan for gold?

"What shall I do? What shall I do?" Jim asked himself over and over again. But no one heard, for his cry was only a whisper.

Jim remembered his mother's parting words. "You are going to a strange country, Jim," she had said. "But remember that the Lord Jesus is just as close to you there as He is at home. You have only to speak to Him and He will hear you. Tell Him if you are hungry. Tell Him if you are lonesome or tired. Tell Him, too, if temptations come to you. He loves you, Jim. He will help you. He will supply your every need. He will keep you from evil. He Himself has promised."

When Jim remembered these words, he took courage. He closed his eyes and prayed, "Dear Lord Jesus, forgive me for not asking what to do. Oh, show me now. Show me what I should do."

Jim opened his eyes slowly. Across the street he saw a man who was dressed like a gentleman. He was walking up and down, swinging a cane and now and then poking at the ground of the corner lot with his cane.

"Maybe this man knows Captain Weatherbee or can tell me where to find him!" Jim thought, brightening. He was about to cross the street when a man in a plaid coat came along and stopped to talk with the man with a cane.

As Jim watched he was astonished to see the man in the plaid coat stealthily reach forth his hand toward the pocket of the other man.

"Hey, mister!" Jim shouted. "You're being robbed!"

The man with the cane, who had been looking toward the lot and waving his cane, turned swiftly. But the man with the plaid coat was gone in a flash. The minute Jim had shouted, he fled into an alley. Jim started after him but he soon saw it was a hopeless chase. The man in the plaid jacket had simply disappeared like the San Francisco fog before the rising sun. It was as if the earth had swallowed him.

"Young man, you have done me a service," a voice said. Jim turned around.

"Oh, excuse me!" said Jim. "I was thinking of that fellow who got away, and didn't see you."

"I'm John Parrott," the man with the cane said as he held out his hand to Jim. "I saw that you were bent on catching him. Tell me, lad, what's your name?"

Jim shook hands with him, replying quickly, "My name is Jim Rogers." Then he added, "And I'm older than I look, I assure you!"

"I'm glad to know you, Jim. I see that you are alert and quick. I could use a—well, a young man like you. How should you like to work for me?"

Jim hesitated. "What kind of work would it be?" he asked.

Mr. Parrott pointed with his cane to the lot across the street. "See that lot, Jim? I'm going to build a business structure on that lot."

Jim looked around at the flimsy stores that had been hastily erected to take care of San Francisco's mushrooming business.

"Nothing like these, Jim," John Parrott said scornfully. Then he added proudly, "I believe in the future of San Francisco. And because I believe in it, I'm going to put up a building that will last. The finest and best in all San Francisco, Jim! It will be built of stones, each one hand-cut. These stones have come from far-off China, brought to San Francisco by sailing vessels. Within a day or so, they will be delivered to my lot here and my workmen will begin their great task of putting them together."

Jim looked at the vacant lot which was on the northwest corner of Montgomery and California Streets. Then he looked at Mr. Parrott who had a far-off look in his eyes as if he had seen a great vision.

Jim smiled. "Do you want me to help put the stones together?"

"No, not that," Mr. Parrott said. "I have a group of skilled carpenters and stoneworkers who will do the work.

What I need is an errand boy. I will pay you forty dollars a month besides your room and board. What do you say, Jim?"

Jim thought of the gold country. But how could he get there without money? Besides, hadn't he prayed to God to help him? And wasn't this an answer to his prayer?

"I'll work for you, Mr. Parrott!" Jim said without further hesitation.

"Good!" said Mr. Parrott as he glanced at his watch. "It's almost lunchtime, Jim. Let's find a place to eat, shall we?"

Between mouthfuls of sizzling steak and fried potatoes, Jim told Mr. Parrott of his sailing on the *Marietta* as cabin boy, of his staying at the lodging house on Montgomery Street and of having all his earnings stolen.

"In fact, sir," Jim said, "I was looking for the captain of the *Marietta* when I saw that fellow in the plaid coat about to rob you."

"What is the name of your captain?"

"Weatherbee. Captain Weatherbee. And a fine man he is, too, Mr. Parrott! He's a man who fears God and who is kind to his crew."

"Weatherbee? That name has a familiar sound. Would your captain be a tall fellow with a growth of black beard?"

"That's the very description of him!" Jim cried eagerly. "You know my captain? Tell me where to find him!"

Mr. Parrott shook his head. "By this time, Jim, he's away up the Sacramento River on his way to the gold country."

"Where did you see him? Tell me!" Jim demanded.

"At the Parker House, Jim," Mr. Parrott chuckled. "If you're looking for someone in San Francisco, wait at the Parker House. Everyone in San Francisco must go there sometime in the day, at least so it seems from the crowds one encounters there."

"Did you talk to him?"

"No. I just heard a steward call his name. And since the man was a striking looking fellow, the name stuck in my mind. I heard the captain say he was going up the river to the gold country that very night."

"And that's where I'd be, too, if my money had not been taken!" Jim said, almost whimperingly. But when he realized that that was no way for a man to act, let alone a Christian, he tried to smile.

"Stay in San Francisco, Jim," Mr. Parrott advised. "You'll do better for yourself in the long run." Then he took five silver dollars from his pocket and handed them to Jim. "Here's an advance on your salary, Jim. You don't want to go around without a penny in your pocket."

That night Jim was glad he had accepted Mr. Parrott's offer of a job when he had a good bed to sleep in and a small room of his own at the back of the house on the ground floor.

The next morning the Chinese cook, Soo Lum Fong, gave Jim a bowl of hot cereal and a jug of cream. Jim took it to his room. He had just settled down to enjoy it when he heard the cook shout, "How about some rolls, boy? Do you want some?"

Jim hurried to the kitchen. He wouldn't miss out on anything so good as hot rolls! Fong was just taking out a pan of rolls from the oven. Their delicious fragrance filled the room. He buttered two and handed them to him. He went back to his room, grateful for the prospect of a fine breakfast. But when he got there, he stared at the table in astonishment. His cereal bowl was empty and the cream had disappeared, too!

He ran out the back door and looked around. But he saw no one. Slowly and reflectively he took his empty bowl and the empty pitcher to Fong and told him what had happened.

Fong laughed till he had to hold his sides. Jim saw that he was so convulsed that the tears ran out of his eyes.

"Why you lie to me, boy?" Fong demanded. "If you want more, say it. Don't tell lies to get it."

There was no use taking any chances with Fong. Perhaps he could not be trusted. Jim had heard tales about the Chinese. Who could tell — maybe they were true?

"I didn't tell a lie, Fong!" Jim said, speaking slowly and deliberately so as not to mock Fong. "I'm a Christian and Christians don't tell lies!"

"That so?" Fong asked, looking intently at Jim.

"Yes, that's so. The Bible says some hard things about liars. And Jesus said the Devil was a liar from the beginning."

"That so?" Fong asked, staring at Jim.

Why did the fellow act so mechanically? Jim wished he knew whether Fong really understood what he was talking about or not.

He tried again. "Fong, it's all true, what I tell you. Adam and Eve knew disobedience of God's word would bring death. And the Devil said, 'God doesn't really mean it. Don't worry, you won't really die!' That was a lie and the Devil knew it was. And that's how death came into the world. Because man believed the Devil's lie rather than God's own word. Now you understand, Fong? I'm telling you about Adam and Eve the first man and the first woman, who believed a lie — long ago in the Garden of Eden."

"Lie bad thing. Velly, velly bad thing." Fong shook his head. "All light, boy, I believe you say tluth. Give me your bowl."

Jim went back to his room and ate his breakfast. He wondered how much good his little talk on lying had done. Oh, well, he could find out later! That evening when Jim came from work, he decided to set a trap for the one who had eaten his cereal. Taking a plate of savory stew to his room, he left it on the table. Then he went out of the room. But he stood in the hall near the door. When he heard a noise, he threw the door open. There, hungrily eating his stew, was a scrawny Chinese boy with a long pigtail down his back.

So this boy was the culprit! What would Jim have to face next?

2

JIM NOTICED that without another glance, the moment that the Chinese boy saw Jim, he ran to the door. Without hesitation Jim ran after him. The Chinese boy was a fast runner, all right! But Jim caught hold of his pigtail and held tight.

"Don't be afraid!" Jim said breathlessly. "I'll not hurt you. What's your name?"

"Lu Chang," the boy replied still looking frightened.

"Where do you live, Lu?" Jim asked, relaxing his hold.

The boy shook his head. "Sleep in alley. Steal food."

"I'm sorry you have no home. But don't you know it's wrong to steal?" Jim asked, not unkindly.

The Chinese boy hung his head. "Lu Chang hungry."

Jim thought quickly. Here was a need, a great need. Maybe Mr. Parrott would let him share his bed with Chang. And maybe he could pay for the food Chang ate out of the forty dollars Mr. Parrott would pay him.

"Don't go away, Lu," Jim said as kindly as he could. "I'm a stranger in San Francisco, too. Maybe we can be friends. Maybe you can stay with me. Would you like that?"

Lu Chang nodded eagerly. "I see you tomorrow? Sleep somewhere tonight, all samee."

Jim didn't question him further. He determined to help this boy.

When Jim asked Mr. Parrott about keeping Lu, Mr. Parrott said, "That's all right if you want to share your bed with Chang but be sure he takes a bath and washes his clothes so that he is clean. And as for his food, he can help Fong in the kitchen and earn his keep that way."

"Thank you, Mr. Parrott! I'm sure you won't regret this help. Lu seems to be a fine boy who hasn't had a chance. He speaks English quite well for one born in China, as he was."

"And you must promise not to steal any more. Do you promise that, Lu Chang?" Jim asked when he saw Lu that very next night.

The Chinese boy nodded eagerly. "Lu Chang work hard. Pay for keep."

"And we'll be friends, Lu?"

"Yes. We friends," Lu agreed.

The first night Jim didn't sleep very well because Lu Chang was restless and woke him up several times by kicking very hard. But after the first night, Jim slept better. Fong said that Lu was a good helper, only he ate more than two or three ordinary boys.

"Never mind," Mr. Parrott said. "After a while Lu will get filled up and then he won't eat so much."

The morning that the workmen were to start on Mr. Parrott's building, Jim went with Mr. Parrott to the lot. It was nine o'clock but already the streets were full of people. There had been fog at seven o'clock when Jim awoke but now the fog was gone, swept away by the invigorating breeze blowing inland from the ocean.

Jim walked briskly alongside Mr. Parrott. They passed busy markets, little groups of men haggling over the price of lots, buying for future speculation. A bit of the conversation was heard as they passed, "Take it or leave it," the seller said, "the price won't come down two bits! Tomorrow it may be twice as much, I warn you!"

Mr. Parrott grinned. "He'd better take it. That's something you learn when you've been in San Francisco for a while. Pay what is asked. If you don't like it, you can leave.

Someone else will buy it. You may as well save your breath for all the good haggling over prices will do you."

"You'd rather be in business in San Francisco than to go to the gold country?" Jim asked.

"I'm in the gold country, Jim! Know how much the Parker House rents for? One hundred and ten thousand dollars a year! And the Parker House is but a shack. Wind whistles through the cracks. But the building John Parrott will erect will be a credit to San Francisco! It will last as long as it is needed and will be here long after John Parrott has gone to his eternal home. Yes, Jim, this building will make history in San Francisco!"

Jim felt a thrill as he listened to Mr. Parrott. This really was history in the making. And he, Jim Rogers, was actually seeing it! San Francisco, a frontier city! And here he was in the very midst of it. Still, it was exciting to dig for gold. Why, any day one might uncover a fortune in the diggings!

When they reached the lot, the workmen were already there. And on the lot were great piles of hand-cut stones which had come all the way from China. Jim saw that the workmen were excited. They were gathered in little groups. Some were arguing. Some were shaking their heads in a hopeless fashion. Jim looked anxiously at Mr. Parrott but Mr. Parrott did not seem troubled.

Jim studied the stones curiously. What odd-looking marks were on them! He could not make out what they were or what they could mean. The workmen, too, were examining the stones. Jim wondered if they had any idea what the markings meant.

Jim spoke to one of the workmen standing by him. "I suppose it's all right if you can read Chinese."

"That's just it," the workman said, "I can't read Chinese and no one else here can read Chinese either. These marks are a puzzle, all right. A Chinese puzzle." He turned to Mr. Parrott. "You'd better get a 'Chink' to figure this out, Boss. It's too much for us."

"Maybe Lu Chang can help us," Jim said hopefully.

Mr. Parrott nodded. "Go and get him, Jim."

Jim ran to Mr. Parrott's house and returned with Lu Chang.

But Lu Chang, too, shook his head.

One by one the workmen began to lay down their tools and leave the lot. Finally only Mr. Parrott, the contractor, Jim, and Lu Chang were left.

Mr. Parrott looked discouraged but the contractor said briskly, "This is a job for Chinese workmen. I'll go and round up some of the China boys. They'll know how to put these stones together."

Away the contractor went and in almost no time was back with a company of Chinese workmen. They, too, examined the stones. But they, too, shook their heads and went away.

"Why you not send for man who make marks on stones?" Lu Chang asked.

"That's just what I'll do!" Mr. Parrott decided. "I'll send to China and have the great architect who designed this building come here and show us how to put it together."

Mr. Parrott did as he said. But there was nothing more to be done until the great Chinese architect arrived in San Francisco.

In the meantime Jim and Lu Chang kept busy in one way or another. Jim considered Lu Chang his special property. Hadn't he caught him by his pigtail? And wasn't he sharing his bed with Lu?

"Tonight we have li-cee," Lu Chang announced in his sing-song tone.

"You mean rice," Jim said.

Lu nodded. "What I say, licee."

"Not licee," Jim corrected. "Rice."

But the letter "r" was something Lu could not always pronounce. Wherever the letter "r" occurred, Lu pronounced it as "l."

"You my fliend," Lu Chang would tell Jim. "You plenty good boy."

"I'm your friend," Jim corrected.

"What I say," Lu returned. "You velly good fliend."

One afternoon Mr. Parrott told Jim and Lu that they could take a holiday. "Let's go down to the ocean," Jim said.

As they were walking along the beach, the tide began to come in and great waves swept the sands of the shore and then receded. Lu fled in terror and did not stop until he was high up on the cliff.

"Look out! Dlagon of the sea will get you!"

"What dragon?"

"He reach for you. Pull you down, down, down!" Lu said.

"There isn't any dragon in the sea. That's only the tide coming in. Come back here." Lu came down shaking his head. "When we come Amelica, we thank gods we escape dlagon."

"There is only one true God, Lu," Jim said.

Lu's eyes widened.

"And there is only one Saviour, the Lord Jesus. Did you know He died for you, Lu?"

Lu stared at Jim in amazement. "For me? Why He die for Lu?"

"To save you, Lu."

"To save me from the dlagon?" Lu asked.

"Well, maybe, but not the dragon you think. But the Devil, he's a dragon, too."

"Tell me, Jim."

"It was this way, Lu. Many, many years ago God created this world. He made everything beautiful. Beautiful flowers, all kinds of trees He made. It was all like a beautiful garden. Then He created a man and a woman and put them in the beautiful garden. God told them they should tend the garden and keep it beautiful. He said that it was theirs and that they could enjoy everything in it.

Only He asked them not to touch the fruit of one tree."

Lu's almond-shaped eyes opened wider. "Did they obey this kind God?"

Jim shook his head. "No, they did not obey Him. So God made them leave the garden. And then things were not beautiful any more. Weeds and briars began to grow where there had been beautiful flowers before. But worst of all because this man and woman did not obey God, disease and death came into the world. Disease and death always follow sin."

"How sad this kind God must be."

Jim nodded. "Yes. He loved this man and this woman and He wanted to save them from sin and death."

"What did He do?" Lu asked.

"A long time later, when the time was right, He sent His Son, the Lord Jesus Christ into the world. He came down to earth to live here and tell us about His home in heaven and about the Father in heaven who loves us. And He said that whoever believed that the Lord Jesus Christ was the Son of God and his own personal Saviour, that person would be saved from sin."

"And not die any more?" Lu asked.

"As long as sin is in the world, death is here. But if you love Jesus you will go to live with God in heaven. You will live forever and ever and you will never be sick there and you will never die."

"I would like to live in heaven," Lu said.

"You can if you take the Lord Jesus Christ as your Saviour," Jim replied.

"And I won't come back in the body of a yellow cat?" Lu asked in wonder.

"No, Lu. People do not come back as cats. When they die they go to heaven or to Hell."

"What's Hell?" Lu asked.

"It is where all the wicked people go."

"I'd rather live in heaven," Lu decided. "I believe this Jesus you tell me about."

"Then you're a Christian, Lu. And before you eat your rice, you must bow your head and say 'Thank you' to your Heavenly Father. And I will read you the Bible every day."

"Heavenly Father," Lu prayed. "No longer am I orphan boy. I have Heavenly Father."

3 JIM AND Lu at last found their time of waiting at an end. There was a great stir and they hurried to find out about it. The great excitement was among the Chinese of San Francisco for the noble architect had arrived from China. This was the great architect who had made the strange markings on the hand-cut stones for Mr. Parrott's building.

Yet the great architect was only a little man. He was dressed in a flowing robe of rich satin and brilliant color. And he walked with dignity. He went at once to the lot where the American, Mr. Parrott, wanted his building. The architect took a ruler from his pocket and began at once to measure the lot. His face was solemn. Everyone watched him as he moved slowly around the lot. The street was full of men from China who had followed the great architect. Jim watched him anxiously.

After the architect had measured the lot carefully, he shook his head. "You must not put your building on this lot," he said to Mr. Parrott. "Evil spirits are here. You must put your building on the lot across the street. There the evil spirits will not bother you."

"But I don't own that lot!" Mr. Parrott objected. "This is my lot. I intend to put the building on this lot."

"Then," the architect said sadly, "I cannot help you. I

cannot put up these stones on a lot where there are evil spirits."

Mr. Parrott pleaded with the great architect. But the architect shook his head and went away. All the men from China who stood by followed the great architect.

The contractor turned to Mr. Parrott. "If you succeed in getting a building on this lot, you'll never get any 'pigtails' into it. Not a 'Chinaman' will ever go through the door."

Jim felt very sorry for Mr. Parrott. But he saw that he was determined to put up the building regardless of what the Chinese said about it.

The next few months were busy ones. Mr. Parrott finally succeeded in getting together a group to work on the building. Mr. Parrott spent long hours studying the markings on the stones, trying to see where they would fit and how to put them together. Finally, the building was finished. It was the first stone building in San Francisco. People of the city called it "Parrott's Castle."

Just as soon as it was ready, two business firms moved into the building.

One was the Adams Express Company and the other was Page, Bacon and Company, bankers.

When the doors were opened for business, not a single Chinese entered the building. It was plain that the Chinese would have nothing to do with "Parrott's Castle." Even the cook, Soo Lum Fong, took his money to the new red brick building across the street which had been built for Wells Fargo and Company.

One day Jim saw Lu Chang in a long line of Chinese waiting patiently for a chance to bank his money with Wells Fargo and Company.

"Why don't you bank in Mr. Parrott's building, Lu?" Jim asked. "You're a Christian now. Surely you don't still believe that there are evil spirits there, do you?"

"Evil spirits, they velly sly," Lu said. "One never know."

Not long after this the steamship *Oregon* sailed into San Francisco Bay bringing news that the eastern office of Page, Bacon and Company had failed. Immediately there was panic in San Francisco. All the banks had long lines of people in front of them, wanting to draw out their money. There were long lines of people in front of Parrott's Castle and there were long lines in front of Wells Fargo and Company.

By this time Jim had been able to save quite a bit of his monthly salary. He had almost three hundred dollars in Page, Bacon and Company. He hurried down to draw his money and received it all. When he returned to his room, Lu Chang was sweeping and dusting.

"You better hurry down to Wells Fargo and Company and get your money, Lu," Jim warned.

"Money safe," Lu said.

Neither Lu nor Fong went to draw their money. "Chinese bank safe," Fong said. Not a single Chinese in all San Francisco went to draw his money from Wells Fargo and Company.

After the panic was over, the people of San Francisco knew that Adams Express had failed and that Page, Bacon and Company had failed. They closed their doors to the public and moved out of Parrott's Castle. The building was now empty. But Wells Fargo and Company were doing a good business.

One day Jim hurried home. He could hardly wait to see Lu. He had the most astonishing piece of news.

"What do you think, Lu? Wells Fargo and Company are moving across the street into Parrott's Castle!"

Lu's brown eyes opened wide with horror. "Where the evil spirits arc?"

Jim chuckled. "They are not afraid of evil spirits. But what are you going to do now, Lu? And what are all the Chinese of San Francisco going to do? Their bank is moving into Parrott's Castle."

Soon all the Chinese had heard the news that their trusted bank was moving into the building haunted by evil spirits. And they began to burn incense to their heathen gods.

In the small room that Jim and Lu occupied together, Lu paced up and down. "Fong goes to offer sacrifices to the God of Wealth," he said.

"What are you going to do, Lu?" Jim asked anxiously. He was afraid that Lu would want to follow Fong.

But Lu smiled. "Lu Christian now. Heavenly Father own all land, all cattle, all wealth. Lu belong Heavenly Father. Lu son of Heavenly Father because he Christian. Heavenly Father all powerful. Lu not aflaid now. Lu walk light in Parrott's Castle, put money in bank!"

Jim grinned. "Good for you, Lu!"

Lu was as good as his word.

Soon other Chinese followed Lu. And then every day long lines of them went in and out of Parrott's Castle.

But one day the cook, Soo Lum Fong, dressed in his best, presented himself to Mr. Parrott. He had drawn out all his money from the bank and he was on his way to the gold fields.

"I'm sorry to lose you, Fong," Mr. Parrott said.

"Lu Chang velly good cook," Fong said. "He makee soup you likee."

Lu Chang was now in the kitchen and he made everything just like Fong had taught him. Mr. Parrott was very satisfied.

Mr. Parrott often entertained. And Lu Chang would serve as well as cook the dinner.

One night Lu said to Jim, "Two men from the gold fields come today. They want young man to help them. You want to go to gold fields? I miss you if you go."

Immediately the longing again took hold of Jim. Mr. Parrott spoke well of Jim to his two friends. They were quite willing to take Jim as partner. So Jim drew out all his savings, outfitted himself, said good-by to Mr. Parrott and Lu Chang and went off to the gold fields with his two partners. It happened just like that!

Up in the beautiful country of the Sierras, Jim panned diligently for gold. He was doing very well. One morning he woke up to smell hot cakes cooking. He jumped out of bed and saw Lu Chang himself bending over the fire!

Jim had missed Lu. Indeed, he was very glad to see him. "Did you come to pan for gold, Lu?"

"No." Lu grinned. "You pan for gold; Lu cook. Lu velly good cook. You pay Lu good wages?"

"Sure thing, Lu!" Jim agreed.

On Sunday Lu said, "Where we go church?"

"There's a church for miners in the village," Jim said.

"Let's go," Lu said.

Jim's two partners, Mike and Sam began to make fun of Jim and Lu for going to church, for they were not Christians.

Lu grabbed the back of the collar of each man. "You come to church, you heathen white men," he said indignantly. "You come to church and you not talk that way."

Mike and Sam were so surprised that they meekly followed as Lu and Jim led the way to the village church. The small building was crowded with miners as Jim hurried his partners down the aisle and Lu brought up the rear. Mike and Sam looked uncomfortable as they had to take their places in the very front row.

"Wish that there preacher wouldn't keep looking at me," Sam complained, wiping his brow with a dirty handkerchief.

Jim knew that the preacher wasn't looking at Sam any more than the rest of the men but he said nothing. No doubt Sam's conscience was beginning to bother him!

The little church rang with the voices of the miners. Jim stole a look at Lu. Lu was singing with his whole heart. Jim was glad that he had been delayed in going to look for gold. If he hadn't been delayed, he wouldn't have met Lu and maybe Lu wouldn't have been a Christian now. And now here was Lu going after Sam and Mike to make Christians of them.

Suddenly a great voice boomed in Jim's ear.

"Would He devote that sacred head
For such a worm as I?"

It was Sam singing! Jim felt a lump in his throat. Why, Sam sang that song as if he knew it! He stole a look at Sam. But Sam's eyes were on the preacher's face. He had seemingly forgotten all about his companions.

The service came to a close. The preacher said, "Anyone who is truly sorry for their sins and would like to begin a new life in the Lord Jesus Christ, just step forward to the altar."

A voice close by said, "How about it, boys? Will you accept God's gift to you?"

Jim looked around. He knew that voice. It was his captain's. It was Captain Weatherbee, all right!

Jim turned and the captain caught him by the shoulder. "Jim Rogers! It's good to see you here. I'm glad that you come to the 'House' of the Lord."

"And it's good to see you, Captain!" Jim then introduced his companions. The Captain inquired closely after the spiritual welfare of each. When he learned that Sam and Mike were not Christians, he said, "Won't you go forward with me and give your hearts to the Lord?"

Sam and Mike both nodded and the great Captain, taking an arm of each, moved forward toward the pulpit. And there and then both Sam and Mike gave their hearts to the Lord.

Afterwards Sam wiped away the tears in his eyes. He told Jim, "My mother used to sing that hymn about the Saviour dying for me but I never gave much heed. She prayed for me though, and she said she would never give up praying for me. Guess her prayers were answered right enough today."

Lu grinned with pleasure. "Likee cook for Sam and Mike now! Likee Christians. We have Christian camp."

"I'm glad you came, Lu Chang," Jim said. "How is Mr. Parrott and how is Parrott's Castle?"

"Both fine," Lu Said. "But Parrott's Castle will last the longest."

And Lu Chang was right. Parrott's Castle on the northwest corner of Montgomery and California Streets was the home of Wells Fargo and Company for more than seventy years.

Christmas at Lone Pine Inn

1 TWELVE-YEAR-OLD Ned Cartwright stood by the front window of Lone Pine Inn and watched the snowdrifts and the flakes sift in powdery mists down the valley and across the mountain. The granite peaks of the Sierras could no longer be seen. Even the dirt road gutted by wagon wheels had disappeared, covered by a blanket of white. Winter had come to the Sierras.

It would be a long winter and a lonely one, thought Ned. And Christmas of the year 1850 was only a few weeks away. It would be a sad Christmas with Father, wasted by typhoid fever, hardly able to leave his bed. A Christmas in a strange inn with strange people — what a prospect! He wished Father had never come to California to look for gold. How much happier they had been in their old home back in Indiana!

Ned turned from the window and looked restlessly around the shadowy general store which occupied most of the lower floor of the inn. The proprietor, Jacob Greene, a gruff man, was at his desk, poring over his books. Jacob Greene had come with his wife, Dorcas, from the State of Maine. Six months they had been in the trading vessel, sailing around the Horn from Boston to San Francisco. Jacob Greene had come, not to dig in the earth for gold, but to take gold from the pockets of men. Already he was rich, supplying the needs of rough-and-ready miners, but charging for food and shelter at an exorbitant cost.

Ned glanced at his ten-year-old sister, Megs. She was sitting in a corner of the store reading a book by an English author named Dickens. The book was *Oliver Twist.* Ned's mother was sewing on a patchwork quilt and by the stove dozed that fiery neighbor, Don Juan Pablo, who had come from old Sonora, Mexico. Only the sounds of his deep-toned snores broke the silence.

Suddenly Don Juan started, his hands clutched his pockets, he gave a long sigh and was wide awake.

With a start Jacob Greene looked up from his books. "What's the matter? Think you've been robbed?" His tone was contemptuous.

A dull red spread over Don Juan's dark face. "I *was* robbed, I tell you! Yellow gold. Four bags of it. I'd know those bags anywhere. Faded blue they were. Made of tent cloth." He clenched his fist. "If I ever find the man . . ." Don Juan drew a knife from his pocket and fingered it.

Jacob Greene shrugged. "'Tain't worth hanging for, Don Juan!"

Don Juan's eyes narrowed. "Just let me find the man!" he muttered, adding a few words in Spanish.

Jacob looked at him. "If you had your gold, you'd have gone to San Francisco," he said scornfully. "You'd have squandered it all by now. And then where'd you be? Like as not you'd be killed. San Francisco's a bad place for a man with gold."

Don Juan fingered his knife and looked sullen.

Ned felt sorry for Don Juan. He had a nice face. He always had been jolly till he lost his gold. Ned pictured him working day after day under the pitiless heat of the valley sun, panning his gold, putting it away in his canvas sacks, waiting till he had enough to return to old Sonora as a wealthy Don. But now his gold was gone. It had been stolen as he slept one night at Lone Pine Inn. And Don Juan had sworn vengeance on the thief.

Suddenly Ned spoke his thoughts aloud. "Christmas is only a few weeks away."

Everyone looked at Ned. Mother stopped sewing. Megs stopped reading. Jacob looked up from his books. Don Juan stared at him. "Noche Buena," Don Juan said softly. Ned knew this was Spanish for Christmas Eve, and that Don probably was thinking of how he had spent Christmas Eve as a boy in Mexico.

"What's Christmas?" Jacob said scornfully. "It's just another day."

Anger swept over Ned. His voice was high-pitched and trembled as he said, "Christmas is *Christmas*. It's not just another day! It's a wonderful day . . ." Tears came to Ned's eyes as he remembered Christmas at home and all the wonderful preparations they had always made for it. He looked at Jacob bent over his books, Jacob who thought Christmas was just another day. "Why, why Christ was born on Christmas Day and He's the Saviour of the world."

"Ned's right," Mother was saying. "Let's make Christmas Day 1850 a Christmas we shall all remember."

"Oh, goody!" Megs cried. "Let's have a Christmas program like those we used to have in Sunday school. Remember, Ned?"

Don Juan sat up and looked interested. "I will play my guitar," he promised.

"And Ned and I will sing," Megs added.

"Don Juan and I can find a little tree, can't we, Don Juan?" Ned asked.

"Maybe," Don Juan agreed.

"When it stops snowing," Mother cautioned.

"Maybe it won't stop," Megs said, looking worried.

Jacob Greene nodded. "Sometimes it doesn't. Not for

days and days." He looked sternly at Mrs. Cartwright. "Your board money doesn't include anything extra, you know!"

Ned saw Mother's face flush. "We'll pay for any extras," she said proudly.

"We'll have a reading of the Scriptures," Ned said. "Papa would like that."

"Maybe Father will be well enough then to come downstairs," Mrs. Cartwright said.

Ned looked around the store. There were barrels of dried fish, pickles, beans, flour and sugar. Some of them were covered now as few people came to trade in the winter. But in the summer dust blew in from the road and swarms of flies crawled unmolested over the open barrels. It would be hard to make the store look Christmasy, Ned thought.

Mrs. Cartwright put her sewing aside. "I'd better see if Father needs anything," she said.

"I'll go, Mama!" Ned said.

Upstairs he tiptoed to Father's room and slowly opened the door. Father looked at him and his gray eyes seemed enormous in his thin, white face.

"It's I, Papa," Ned said.

His father seemed to relax. "Come in, Ned," he said weakly.

Ned drew up a chair to the bed. "Do you want anything, Papa?"

Father shook his head. "No." His hand stole under his pillow and he drew out a small canvas bag. "Ever since Don Juan's gold was stolen, I worry about this gold."

"But there's no one at the inn now, Papa, but Jacob and Dorcas and Don Juan," Ned said.

Father nodded. "I know. But even so, I worry."

"Maybe if you trusted God, Papa?" Ned said in a low tone.

Father closed his eyes and tears stole out under the lids. "Thank you, son. In my weakness I forgot. You are right. I *must* trust God!" He sighed, then added, "Jacob Greene is a hard man, Ned. I don't doubt that he'd put us out if we did not have the gold to pay."

"In the winter?" Ned asked. "With you sick, Papa? Why, where'd we go?"

"That's just it," his father said. "That's why I'm worried. That's why this little bag of nuggets is so important. They must keep us through this winter. In the spring we'll start fresh again. In the spring, I feel sure, I will make a fortune."

"Christmas is only a few weeks away, Papa."

"Why, that's so, it is," Father answered. "I had forgotten. I had forgotten Christmas. I have no gift for you, no gift for any of you. What shall I do?"

"I know a gift you can give us, Papa," Ned said, his voice excited.

"What is that, son?"

"To be well! That is what we want more than anything."

Mr. Cartwright patted Ned's hand. "You are a good son, Ned. I will try to give you the present you wish. I will try."

"Then you must begin by eating some supper, Papa."

Father wrinkled his nose. "What is it? Beans again?"

Ned sighed. "Some broth for you, Papa, made from meat. And Mama says she will make you a dessert if you'll eat all your broth." He wouldn't worry his papa by saying that Mama would have to pay extra for the dessert.

Father sighed, and whispered, "I'll try, my son."

When Ned came downstairs he heard a great commotion. Two men had come into the store, stamping the snow from their boots, demanding food and shelter. One of them had a scar, and thick matted black hair. The other had a rough beard and long hair. The one with black hair was called Black Boris and the other, Prince Charlie.

When Mother slipped out to the kitchen, Ned and Megs

followed her. Jacob's wife, Dorcas, was stirring the fried beans. When she heard of Black Boris and Prince Charlie, she held up her hands. "'Tis rumored they are robbers. What ill fate has brought *them* to this door?"

Ned thought of Father's little bag of gold and trembled. "Dear Lord," he whispered, "don't let them get Papa's gold."

2

THE DAYS before Christmas were getting fewer. The morning after the arrival of Black Boris and Prince Charlie, the snow stopped and by noon the sun shone. The sky was blue. Ned looked out with delight on a world of fresh, untrampled snow. The majestic snow-capped peaks of the Sierras were an awesome sight against the blue backdrop of the sky. The pines and the cedars and the firs were heavily laden with snow.

Ned sighed with pleasure. "Why it feels like Christmas already!"

Megs sniffed. "I smell flapjacks. I'm hungry."

At lunch the talk centered on the exciting news that Black Boris and Prince Charlie had brought. California had been admitted to the Union as a state. Black Boris and Prince Charlie had been in San Francisco when the news came through on the morning of October 18. Such a celebration they had never seen.

The people had thrown business to the winds. Everybody celebrated. And at night there had been a great gathering in Portsmouth Square. The next morning Governor Burnett had left by stage for San Jose, driving at a fast pace. The news had been shouted all along the way to the astonished people who flocked to the roadside: "California has been admitted to the Union as a state."

"Yes, sir," Black Boris said, "Eighteen-fifty is a year California will long remember!"

"Is it true that there are about twenty thousand people in San Francisco now?" Mrs. Cartwright asked.

"Yes, ma'am," Prince Charlie replied. "All of that. I'd say there's nearer twenty-five thousand."

"Two years ago there weren't even two hundred," Jacob Greene put in.

Ned listened with fascination. Some day he would go to San Francisco and see that great city for himself.

Black Boris told of the hundreds of ships which lay in San Franciso Bay, deserted by their crews who had all gone off to the "diggings."

The days passed and Prince Charlie and Black Boris still behaved themselves very well. Ned began to like them and to think that Dorcas had been wrong when she said they were robbers. He would have continued to think so if Mother had not lost her gold locket.

The locket was one she greatly treasured. As she was in the habit of wearing it each day, she seemed to remember putting it on the morning that it had disappeared. But Don Juan said that it had probably been stolen as she slept, even as his bags of gold had been stolen.

But Mrs. Cartwright thought it had become unclasped and slipped from her neck. Black Boris and Prince Charlie seemed concerned at the loss and went searching the store for it.

"Humph!" Dorcas said, eyeing them suspiciously. To Ned she said, " 'Tis a pretty game they play and all the time they have the locket!"

"Oh," Ned said in surprise, "do you think they took Mama's locket?"

"Of course they did! They're robbers. You can tell from looking at them. But your Mama had better be careful what she says. Like as not they'd cut our throats while we sleep if they thought we suspected them."

So no one said anything at all to Prince Charlie and Black Boris about their being suspected of having stolen the gold locket. But Papa worried more than ever about his rapidly decreasing bag of nuggets.

Yet Black Boris and Prince Charlie *were* entertaining talkers. One evening they told of their stake along the American River. In just a few days they had taken out twenty thousand dollars in gold. Old Jacob listened greedily. Black Boris drew out a bag from his pocket and showed them some gold slugs, hexagonal in shape, worth fifty dollars each. They had been minted at Bear Valley.

Don Juan looked sad as he eyed the gold. No doubt he was thinking of his that had been stolen.

After this, Jacob whimpered more than ever at the high cost of everything. Ned knew that he would charge Black Boris and Prince Charlie as much as he dared. "A dollar and a half for a pound of flour. Three dollars for a pound of brown sugar!" Jacob groaned as he muttered the words under his breath.

In disgust, Black Boris threw two gold slugs on Jacob's desk. "Take that and stop your growling!" he said.

Jacob's fingers closed over the gold.

But when Jacob was not around, Black Boris told of paying three dollars for a square meal at the El Dorado Hotel in Hangtown and that he knew a miner who'd paid eighteen dollars for a pair of boots.

Each night after supper Ned and Megs would have Bible reading and prayer with Mother and Father upstairs. They would draw their chairs close to Papa's bed and then kneel on the floor beside it. They could often hear the sounds of swearing, cursing, and loud talking floating up from the lower floor. Sometimes they heard Don Juan play his guitar.

Looking up from the Bible reading that same night, Megs said, "Oh, I've the best idea ever for our Christmas Day program! Ned and I could make little scenes of the Christmas story. We could do one of the shepherds in the field and Mama could be the angel. She could say, 'Fear not: for, behold, I bring you good tidings of great joy, which shall be to all people. For unto you is born this day in the city of David a Saviour, which is Christ the Lord.' Would you do it, please, Mama?"

Mrs. Cartwright smiled as she answered, "Yes, I will do it."

"And we could have the scene of the inn where the innkeeper would tell Joseph gruffly that there was no room for them at the inn." Megs giggled. "We better let Jacob Greene do *that* part! He'd fit it just right!"

Mrs. Cartwright looked at Megs reprovingly. "For shame, Megs!"

"Megs is right, Mama," Ned said as he defended his sister. "I do think that Jacob is as hard as that innkeeper."

Mother shook her head. "But you'll not get Jacob to take part in a Christmas scene."

"I know that, Mama," Ned said. "I'll be the innkeeper and I'll act just like Jacob."

"Maybe Dorcas will help in one of the scenes," Mrs. Cartwright suggested. "She's a Christian."

"Yes, Mama, ever since that circuit riding missionary stayed here that night, Dorcas has been different. She got right down on her knees and said she was a sinner and she needed a Saviour," Ned said.

"But Jacob got mad as anything when the missionary said *he* was a sinner!" Megs put in. "His face got red and he said he didn't have any sins he needed to confess," Megs added.

"The Bible says we are all sinners and we all need the Lord Jesus to be our Saviour," Mrs. Cartwright said. "We must pray for Jacob and not criticize him."

But the next time that Mama took the gold nuggets to pay Jacob for their room and board, Jacob told her gruffly that it wasn't enough. He would have to charge them more.

Papa groaned in despair when he heard this. "Our gold will not last," he said. "What shall we do?"

"Don't worry," Mama assured him. "Jacob can't put us out in the snow."

"He would do it," Mr. Cartwright muttered. "He's a hard man."

Mother looked worried. Later she said to Ned, "We must do something to cheer Papa. Otherwise, he will not get better. We want him to be well so that when spring comes we can go back to our mine."

"But will he be well enough to work the mine, Mama?" Megs asked.

"I can help him," Ned said. "I'm well and strong. I can work." Ned had no sooner said these words than an idea came to him. The more Ned thought of it, the better it seemed to him. He'd speak to Jacob and offer his services. He could scrub and sweep, set the table and wash dishes.

When Ned had decided, he had a talk with Mama. She did not like the idea of Ned working for Jacob. But finally she came to see that there was no other way out.

But Jacob was not inclined to take on any worker. "We're getting along fine. I can't afford to pay wages to a laborer."

"You don't need to pay any wages," Ned said eagerly. "Just let us stay here until spring."

Jacob finally agreed that Ned could work for his own room and board. When Ned told Papa, he nodded and said, "You must take a man's part, Ned. You are a good boy and I'm proud of you."

Ned was happy when he saw how much happier Papa looked. "I'm sure now," Mrs. Cartwright said, "that our gold will carry us through the winter."

But Ned knew that old Jacob would make him work as hard and as fast as ever he could.

3 IT WASN'T easy for Ned to work for old Jacob. He was a hard taskmaster. There were jobs that hadn't been done for months — jobs like cleaning off all the shelves and arranging the stock. There were hard jobs, too, like scrubbing the floors, the table, and the counters. Ned's hands were sore and his back ached. But he did not complain. He worked willingly. Ned didn't want Father to know that he worked so hard. He made him think he really enjoyed it.

Ned saw that even old Jacob was surprised at his work. When he had been especially mean and Ned shut his lips tight and never answered him back an angry word, Ned could see that old Jacob was looking at him with a puzzled frown. Plainly old Jacob could not understand it all. But if Black Boris or Prince Charlie heard old Jacob speak harshly to Ned or hurry him with his impossibly hard tasks, they spoke sharply to the old fellow. So Jacob was careful not to be mean to Ned when they were around.

Even Don Juan would look with an ugly glance at old Jacob if he happened to be around and heard him abuse Ned. But as the days passed Don Juan slept most of the time that he spent at the store. The heart had gone out of him because his gold had been stolen and he was no longer ambitious. Besides, the stove was making the store a warm place to stay!

Don Juan had been one of a small group of Mexicans who had settled in the center of a little valley in California. They called their village, Campo de Sonora, after their beloved Mexican state. The little settlement was well situated in a grassy oak-dotted valley between two streams. Here the Mexicans enjoyed their sleepy little settlement. But not for long.

On January 24 in the year 1848, gold had been discovered by James Marshall during the excavation for a sawmill which he was building in partnership with John Sutter. The sawmill was on the American River about eighty-six miles north of Sonora. It took time for the news to get around but by 1849 the great California gold rush was on. At the end of 1849 Campo de Sonora was no longer a sleepy little Mexican village but the booming town of Sonora. Population leaped to fourteen thousand, of which ten thousand were Mexicans.

Don Juan had been successful. He had found a pocket of gold, a rich deposit. But first his partner had cheated him. And now his little remaining store of gold had been stolen. Just a few weeks ago four bags of it had disappeared while he slept at Lone Pine Inn. Gone were his dreams of a return to old Sonora to live the life of a rich Don.

The day before Christmas dawned cold but clear. A fire burned brightly on the hearth at the sitting room of the inn. Ned looked around the store part. It was clean and tidy except for one corner where there were sacks of grain and heavy barrels. Old Jacob had ordered that they should not be moved. But Ned wondered what harm it would do to straighten them out.

Old Jacob was dozing in the kitchen. Black Boris and Prince Charlie had gone in search of a little fir tree and some greens to hang over the doorway and the windows. Megs was busily writing out their Christmas program. Mother was sewing on her patchwork quilt. Upstairs Father slept. No one was in the storeroom but Don Juan, and he was asleep.

Ned couldn't move the barrels by himself. He went over to Don Juan and began to shake him. "Wake up, Don Juan. I want you to help me."

The Mexican gasped as Ned shook him. He reached for his knife.

"It's I, Ned, Don Juan!"

Shamefacedly Don Juan put away his knife.

"Come help me move these barrels!" Ned ordered.

Reluctantly Don Juan rose to his feet. Mechanically he obeyed Ned's order, shoving the barrels and sacks where

Ned directed. "That's fine, Don Juan! Now I'll sweep it out here. Then I'll call you again and you can help me shove back this stuff."

Don Juan stumbled back to his chair. In a moment he was fast asleep. Ned swept the floor. As he stooped to sweep the dirt onto a shovel, he noticed a wide crack in the floor. He looked more closely and saw that it was a trap door in the floor. Curiously, he swung it up. An exclamation of surprise broke from his lips. He looked up startled but Don Juan slept on.

Ned stared into the shallow cache and at the sacks piled there. He touched one of them experimentally. Gold! Gold worth thousands and thousands of dollars! Fascinated, he knelt there, gazing at the treasure he had so unexpectedly uncovered. Then he trembled. The sacks were different. Among them there were four blue ones. Don Juan had said his sacks were made from old tent cloth, faded blue tent cloth. Yes, in the cache were four bags, bags of faded blue tent cloth!

Ned picked up one of the bags and then almost dropped it, he was so astonished. The bag had been on top of a small box. The box was open. It was full of jewelry, gold rings, and necklaces. Among them Ned saw Mother's locket.

Ned hesitated. Should he take the locket? If he did, Jacob would know that someone had discovered the cache. No, it was better not to risk it.

Ned looked up at Don Juan, asleep in his chair. Should he show Don Juan the gold? Ned remembered Don Juan's knife and his threat to kill the man who had stolen his gold. Maybe Don Juan would make good his threat. Maybe he would kill old Jacob.

Then Ned heard Black Boris and Prince Charlie approaching the inn. Quickly he shut the trap door and pushed some old sacks over it. Just in time! Black Boris and Prince Charlie came stamping in. Black Boris cried,

"Here's a fine little fir for you, Ned! 'Twill make a jolly Christmas."

"And here's some green," Prince Charlie said.

Don Juan woke up when he heard all the noise. After praising the little tree Black Boris had found and admiring the green, Ned motioned to Don Juan. Yawning and stretching, Don came over and helped Ned push the sacks and barrels back in place.

While he helped with the Christmas decorations, Ned's mind was on the bags of gold he had uncovered. What should he do about his discovery? His fear was that Don Juan might do something dreadful to old Jacob when he discovered that he was the one who had stolen his gold. Ned remembered the times old Jacob had twitted Don Juan, saying that his gold was only a figment of his imagination.

Ned didn't want to worry Father and Mother. He was afraid that Dorcas' story about Black Boris and Prince Charlie might be true. If they were robbers then Don Juan's gold would surely be lost. Still, they had not stolen the locket as Dorcas thought. It was old Jacob! And Ned was sure that good Dorcas who worked so hard and was so kind, was entirely ignorant of old Jacob's theft.

What should he do? Ned turned the question over and over in his mind. Then suddenly, he remembered — why he could tell it all to the Lord Jesus! The Lord would show him what to do. Didn't the Bible say that if any one lacked wisdom he should ask of God and He would show him what to do? Why, here he had been carrying this heavy burden, worrying what to do, when all that was necessary was to ask the Lord Jesus what to do and He would show him!

When the decorations were completed, old Jacob came and stood in the doorway. "What goes on here?" he roared.

"It's Christmas, sir!" Ned said.

"Christmas!" muttered old Jacob. "What's Christmas?"

Dorcas stood behind old Jacob. "For shame, Jacob! Do you think of nothing but making money?"

"What else is there to think of?" Jacob asked, a sour look on his face.

"There's plenty, sir!" Ned replied. "If you die you'll leave all your gold here. You can't take it with you, sir."

Jacob's face was purple with rage. "Get busy, boy! Set the table in the kitchen."

Dorcas put her arm over Ned's shoulder in a kind way. "Come along, Ned. We'll go together."

Ned set the table thoughtfully. He felt sorry for poor Dorcas. She was honest and kind. She did not know that old Jacob had stolen Don Juan's gold. She thought Prince Charlie and Black Boris were thieves but they were honest men. Ned was *sure* of that!

Ned knew he must think of a way to get Don Juan's gold back to him and to keep him from getting angry with old Jacob. How could he do it?

After supper Ned washed the dishes. Then old Jacob ordered him to scrub the kitchen floor. Ned cheerfully agreed. When the others left the room, Jacob loitered. He looked at Ned with the puzzled expression that was often on his face when he regarded him. Had he found that Ned swept the corner?

"You're a queer boy, Ned," he said. "You act like you enjoyed doing all the hard tasks I put on you."

Ned looked up. Then he grinned. "What good would it do not to enjoy them?" he asked cheerfully. "Besides, I was reading in the Scriptures where it said, 'he who would be great among you, let him be your servant.' The Lord Jesus took on Himself the form of a servant. And besides, sir," Ned added, looking into old Jacob's eyes, "any honest work is good. I want to always earn my way by *honest* work!" Unconsciously Ned straightened.

Jacob fell back, his face scarlet.

Ned looked at him in surprise, then said, " 'Tis a wicked thing to steal."

Jacob looked frightened. Then with a muttered oath, he turned and left the room.

Ned looked after him thoughtfully. Old Jacob's conscience was hurting him. That was sure. Suddenly Ned clapped his hands. He had an idea, a wonderful idea of a way to get Don Juan's gold back to him. He'd carry it out tomorrow, on Christmas Day.

4

ON CHRISTMAS Day there was a great storm. The wind roared around Lone Pine Inn. The trees whipped back and forth in the gale. Snow in powdery mists swept across the foothills, hiding the High Sierras from view.

The storm made Lone Pine Inn a welcome shelter even though the cold wind sifted through the cracks in the wall. A cheerful fire blazed on the hearth. Dorcas had planned a Christmas feast of venison, fried corn meal mush, bacon, beans, and salt pork, and an apple pie made with dried apples.

Ned waited, his pulses throbbing with excitement. How would his plan work? He was glad that his part in the program came before dinner. Then, with his responsibility behind him, he could enjoy the Christmas feast.

Ned was happy to see that Papa was well enough to get up. He had made good his promise of getting better by Christmas and he joined the others around the blazing hearth.

The store and inn looked Christmasy and it smelled Christmasy, too, with the fragrant boughs of fir and pine and the cheerful little Christmas tree.

Ned looked over the group gathered before the fire. There were Mama, and Papa, and Megs, good Dorcas and greedy old Jacob. There was Don Juan, awake and interested for he was to entertain them with his guitar. There were rough Boris and long-haired Prince Charlie.

"Now, Papa," Ned said, "please read the Christmas story in the second chapter of Luke's Gospel."

Everyone listened carefully, Ned noticed. Only old Jacob stirred uncomfortably.

Then Megs and Ned pretended they were shepherds on the hillside who heard the announcement of the angel that a Saviour for mankind was born in the city of David.

After this it was time for Ned's plan. He was the innkeeper who had turned away Mary and Joseph because there was no room for them at the inn. Ned walked back and forth, rubbing his hands together, saying, "This taxation has been a great thing for me. Why, it has brought hordes of people. The money has poured in. Right now, I've hidden away bags of money under this very floor I'm walking on."

Ned looked at old Jacob and saw him start as if he would jump to his feet. Then he thought better of it and clung to his chair. He was shaking and his face was white. But no one noticed Jacob. Their eyes were on Ned as he continued, "Ha! I would not like to tell just how I came by that money . . ."

When Ned's little scene was finished, he sat down and his audience clapped generously. Megs leaned over and whispered, "That was old Jacob true enough, Ned. I wonder if he recognized himself."

Ned glanced over at Jacob and the innkeeper was looking at him with fear in his eyes.

After this Don Juan entertained with his guitar. He played old Spanish airs, then a popular song entitled "Oh! Susanna." Everyone joined in singing this song as it was popular with the miners.

Then Papa led in the singing of hymns. To everyone's surprise Prince Charlie sang the hymns, too, knowing every word. Black Boris wiped his eyes with a rough hand.

When the program was finished, Dorcas hurried out to the kitchen where she had made ready their Christmas feast. Everyone followed her out except Jacob who caught at Ned's coat. "Stay!" he demanded.

Ned stayed and the others passed on into the kitchen. Old Jacob beckoned Ned to a far corner of the store and then said in a broken voice, "You . . . you know about the gold?"

Ned nodded, saying tremblingly, "Yes, I know."

Jacob wrung his hands. "What shall I do? Don Juan will kill me if he finds out. Promise to keep this to yourself and I'll let you off working for me. Your family can stay here the rest of the winter and I'll give you whatever you want!"

Ned felt sorry for old Jacob. Even now he was trying to find a way to keep on with his evil deeds. He shook his head. "No, Jacob! You must give back Don Juan's gold and any other that you have taken. You must give the locket back to Mama, too."

Jacob trembled. "Dorcas' heart will be broken. I'm afraid too of Black Boris and Prince Charlie. I'm afraid of Don Juan."

"You should have thought of that before you stole the gold," Ned said. He considered. "Do you truly repent, Jacob?"

Jacob nodded. "I repent."

"Will you give Don Juan's gold back and Mama's locket?"

Jacob bowed his head. "Yes!" he said.

"Let me plan, then, Jacob. Maybe Dorcas and the others need not know." Ned did not want poor Dorcas to know the truth about Jacob as he knew it would make her very unhappy.

Jacob looked at Ned gratefully. "You're sure Don Juan won't kill me?"

"I'm not sure," Ned said, "but I'll do what I can."

Jacob agreed and the two of them went into the kitchen for the Christmas feast.

After they had eaten, Don Juan strummed again on his guitar. He looked happy and for the time being seemed to have forgotten about his stolen gold.

Ned had to wait some time before he could be alone with Don Juan. Then he said, "Christmas is a wonderful day, Don Juan. God gave His Son to us to save us from sin."

Don Juan nodded.

"When God was so good to us to send his only beloved Son to be our Saviour, don't you think we ought to love and to forgive one another?"

Don Juan agreed, "Si, si."

Ned drew a deep breath. "Suppose, Don Juan, the Lord should restore your gold to you."

Don Juan touched his knife. "My gold? My gold? Where is it?"

"Put away your knife, Don Juan, if you want your gold returned. Take it and say nothing. Do you promise?"

"If I get my gold back, I will take it and say nothing," Don Juan said, his eyes glowing with excitement.

"That is a promise?"

"It is a promise."

Ned hurried into the kitchen and called, "Jacob, come now."

In the store, old Jacob began to push away the sacks of grain and the barrels which covered the trap door. Don Juan hurried to help him. Old Jacob lifted the door and drew out, one at a time, Don Juan's four blue bags filled with gold. Don Juan took them and pressed them to his heart. Then Jacob gave the gold locket to Ned.

"I've been a wicked and sinful man," Jacob said.

But Don Juan was so happy to have his gold back that he hardly heard him. He smiled at old Jacob. "In the spring, Don Juan will return to old Sonora, to live his life to a ripe old age."

Then Jacob went to the kitchen and called Dorcas. "Dorcas," he said, "you can put that sampler over the fireplace now."

"Ay, Jacob, that's the best Christmas present I ever had." Dorcas was beaming as she hung the framed sampler she had embroidered with her own hands. Ned read the words, "Christ is the Head of this house."

Then Jacob turned to Ned. "I've charged your papa too much. You need not work for me any more. I will make it good with him."

"Oh, I like to work!" Ned said. "I'm an able-bodied boy, not far from being a man. Why should you and old Dorcas have all the work to do?"

Jacob looked happy. "You are a good boy, Ned. You shall continue to work for me. But I shall pay you wages for your work."

As they gathered round the fireplace, Prince Charlie broke out singing and they all joined in the carol:

"God rest you merry, gentlemen,
Let nothing you dismay,
Remember, Christ our Saviour
Was born on Christmas Day
To save us all from Satan's power
When we were gone astray;
O tidings of comfort and joy.

"From God our Heavenly Father
A blessed angel came;
And unto certain shepherds
Brought tidings of the same;
How that in Bethlehem was born
The Son of God by name
O tidings of comfort and joy."

When Ned's family went upstairs, Papa said, "I have

made great strides in recovery of my health even this day. It has been a good Christmas."

Megs sighed. "Yes, even if we did not have gifts for one another, it was a good day."

Here Ned spoke up. "I have a gift for you, Mama. It is your locket which Jacob gave to me this very day."

"Oh, he found it! How wonderful!"

Ned knew that it would never occur to her that Jacob had stolen it.

"Papa's recovery is a gift to us all," Megs said softly. "We are very fortunate."

"Yes," Mr. Cartwright nodded. "I feel that I can make a fresh start when spring comes. Black Boris and Prince Charlie have promised to help me. They are kind men even if they are rough miners."

"And old Jacob's change of heart," Ned reminded them. "Now he will pay me wages," Ned said. But he did not tell them about the gold and the locket that old Jacob had stolen and returned. He would never mention that. Ned felt a warm happiness deep down in his heart. Christmas 1850 had been a good Christmas. He would *always* remember it!